W9-BHU-474

The very gorgeous

Miss Cannelli — goddess of 5/6c

For Gig

With thanks to the teachers for the fun,
and for telling me stories

Published by
Dell Yearling
an imprint of
Random House Children's Books
a division of Random House, Inc.
1540 Broadway
New York, New York 10036

Visit us on the Web! www.randomhouse.com/kids

Educators and librarians, for a variety of teaching tools, visit us at www.randomhouse.com/teachers

ISBN: 0-440-41652-3

Reprinted by arrangement with Alfred A. Knopf, a division of Random House, Inc.

Printed in the United States of America

June 2001

10 9 8 7 6 5 4 3 2 1

OPM

Don't Pat the Wombat!

by Elizabeth Honey

A Yearling Book

illustrated by Gig

CONTENTS

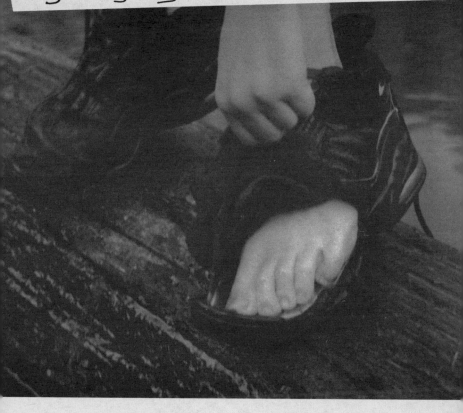

Brought to you by our sponsor Nuke Fresh Air ©

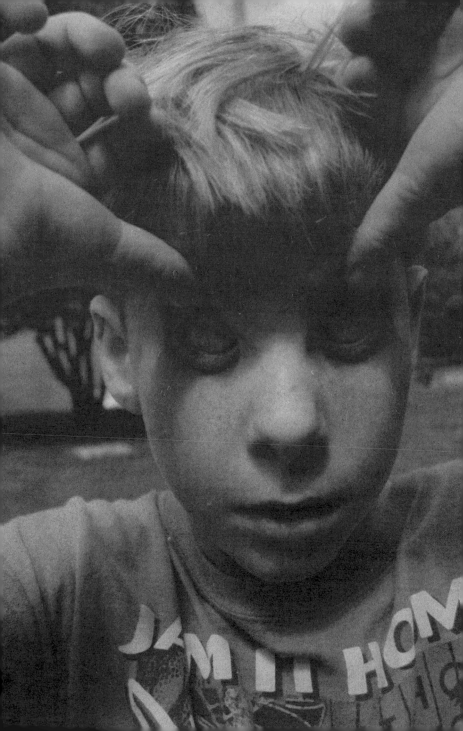

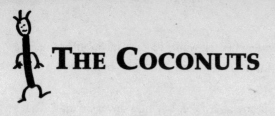# THE COCONUTS

The Coconuts. Mum gave us that name one sunny day, rattling along all squashed into our old bomb.

"I've got a lov-er-ly bunch of coconuts," she sang at the top of her voice.

So now you know what Mum's like.

As for the rest of us, I made friends with Wormz at preschool, except in those days he was called Dear Little Michael. I remember we built a cubby with some boards behind a bush. It was a great success because it had a big daddy-longlegs spider at the back. Bunches of kids used to squeeze in, see the spider, then rush out screaming, "Spideeeeeee! Spideeeeeee! Spideeeeeee!" And we would stay in the cubby, even though the spider was still there. We never told them it was dead.

Also, you know how they make you have a sleep? Well, Wormz and me never wanted to have a sleep. We would lie on our mats beside each other and play winking games.

Wormz wears his sisters' hand-me-down clothes, even though sometimes they're verging on the girl look. The label on his windcheater says Tessa Merlino. I guess his mum is trying to get the clothes worn out.

He wasn't in my class last year. (They split you up from your friends.) But this year we are in grade six together, which is extremely cool.

His great toothy grin is the inspiration for the front of Luna Park. Everyone's hoping his head will grow to fit his teeth. I reckon he has to concentrate when he wants to keep his mouth shut. The Merlinos laugh a lot. His mum and dad run a bulldozer business called Easy Doze It.

Wormz is as skinny as a rake, but he's always eating. That's why he's called Wormz. His life slips along easily. You can't help being friends with Wormz. He'll be friends with anybody.

Then there's Nicko. Real name: David Nicholson. Nicko is the storyman. The only one who brought books to camp. He brought his favorite Little Golden Book, *Mickey Mouse and His Spaceship,* a John Marsden book, and everything in between. Favorite author: everybody. Nicko has read every *Goosebumps* book there is, and has shaken hands with a person who has shaken hands with a person who has shaken hands with a person who has shaken hands with a man who once cut Roald Dahl's hair.

Nicko lives near us, and he stayed with us for a whole month when his parents visited his gran in Canada.

Mitch. Real name: Fawkner A.* Mitchell. Rich Mitch.

*He won't tell us what the A stands for.

His haircuts cost $60 and his Nike Air Max 3's cost over $200 in America. He came to our school in grade two, I think. I remember how he looked because his clothes were so new. He didn't make any friends. Then he turned up with a new ball.

"Do you want to play with my ball?"

The kids played with his ball, but they still didn't play with him. They said he was stuck-up, and he got in trouble for being a bully.

Then he wasn't in my class again until grade five. He has changed. He's much better. He doesn't always have to *have* everything and be best and first all the time. He still *does* have everything, and he can be a pain, but he can also be wickedly funny. His mum does his projects.

The Mitchells live in a fancy new architect house with windows down to the floor. When it was finished, Mitch's dad put multicolored party lights and plastic furniture round the pool. The architect had a nervous breakdown.

Always have something to eat before you nick over to Mitch's house for a go on his computer. The first time I went there: "No, no, no! Don't touch those chocolate cookies! They're Mum's."

"How about those peanuts?"

"No, no, no! They're Dad's."

"Well, can we have this little packet of Shapes?"

"No, no, no! They're just for school lunches."

"What about these raisins?"

"No, no, no! They're for cooking."

Get the picture?

Azza is very simple. Real name: Mario Azzami. I think he hatched out of a basketball. We love basketball. He lives basketball. He always has a ball in his hand...*boing*...*boing*...*boing*...bouncing it off a seat, door, fire hydrant, tree, pedestrian, *boing*...*boing*...*boing*...*boing*...*boing*...*boing*...*boing*...

He doesn't have to look when he bounces. He was born with an invisible ball magnet in his hand. The ball automatically comes back to it. He shoots for goal, and six times out of five it's a swish! Needless to say, he's captain of the basketball team.

And if he's not bouncing a basketball, he's throwing a stick, a rock, or something. He's won stacks of things for sport. He's fast in some ways, but he's slow in others, like writing and math. He is also fantastic at sound effects, which adults describe as "annoying noises."

Then there's me, Mark Ryder. Nickname: Exclamation Mark. No prize for guessing why!!!!!!! Most Unimproved Player of the Year (but best writer!).

So now you know what we're like. We aren't an exclusive club or anything, we've just been friends for a long time. We muck around together and stay at each other's houses and stuff. At school we're the funny ones. If Miss Cappelli wants someone to do something crazy, she picks one of us. In the Cinderella assembly, we were all ugly sisters.

Then along comes Jonah.

Mitch didn't like Jonah much, which is funny, because for a long time Mitch didn't fit in very well either.

2 TWO THINGS

Two things happened the month before school camp: Jonah suddenly arrived in our class, and Mum gave me her old camera for my birthday.

Jonah was there on a Monday morning, sitting in the back with a blank look on his face. He wasn't shy, but he wasn't smiley want-to-be-my-friend either. He wore a black hat with a brim. Not a school hat or a Crocodile Dundee hat. Like this: and daggy overalls with lots of pockets, and a daggy dark purple jacket.

Miss Cappelli made a little mime to him to take his hat off. He put it on the desk in front of him.

"We've got a new member in our class. Stand up, Jonah. Jonah comes from up near Tubbut."

He stood looking out the window.

"Tubbut's up in the northeast, near...what's it near, Jonah?"

He shrugged. "It's not near anything."

"Azza, will you *stop* making that Velcro noise with your shoe. Jonah's come from a little school to our big school. Welcome to 5/6C, Jonah. I guess you're feeling a bit strange, but we're a friendly lot. You'll certainly get to know everyone at camp."

We stared at him, but he didn't look at anybody or anything. He stood as if his mother was trying on him some new clothes that he couldn't care less about. Or as if he was trapped in an invisible force field.

Beth the Good, whose dad works in the post office, whispered, "In the Bible, Jonah got swallowed by a whale!"

"Where's his whale?" sniggered Tommo loudly.

"I'd like you to make Jonah welcome," says Miss Cappelli, glaring at Tommo. So we give Jonah a clap like we always do to show our appreciation, or welcome, or any stupid thing. He wasn't the sort of person to clap. Anyway, the clap bounced off Jonah like rain off a tin roof.

"Pete and Tak, could you show Jonah around at lunchtime, please?"

Then we got on with our work.

At lunchtime, Pete says to Jonah, "I'll show you where the toilets are."

"No, it's okay, I'll go with them," says Jonah, pointing to us. And that's how he came to be a Coconut.

❢❢❢❢❢

Now I'll tell you about the camera. It doesn't sound like much, getting your mum's old camera for your birthday, but it's a Pentax. This is a big deal, even if it has a dint in the viewfinder where Mum dropped it. She bought a new camera and had the old camera repaired. You should see some of the black-and-white photos she took with it. There's one in our kitchen of our old dog leaping down from a fence. It's fantastic!

Mum showed me how to take photos. If you let in too much light, the photo is all white. Not enough light, and the photo is black. And you have to get it in focus, otherwise the photo looks like you took it through a shower curtain.

"I'm taking my camera to school camp," I said.

Mum looked a bit unsure. "It's a good camera, you know."

12

"I'll look after it."

Then she decided it was worth the risk. "I'd love to see some photos of camp. I'll give you a roll of film."

"Black-and-white?"

"If that's what you want."

"I do."

Too much light

Not enough light

Out of focus

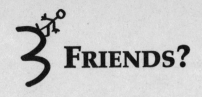 3 FRIENDS?

So Jonah attached himself to us, although he didn't seem to need anybody. I think he thought it was the easiest thing to do. He was so quiet, and we were so "us."

"Why did you leave your farm?" Nicko asked.

"We had to."

"Why?"

"Bad luck."

"Like, your dad lost all your money at the casino?"

"No. We didn't sell the bullocks at the right time, then it didn't rain. The prices dropped, and we ran out of feed."

"That's a great heap of bad luck!" said Wormz. "What happened to the bullocks?"

"We trucked them to my uncle's farm and sold our farm."

"Gee…that must have been so bad."

He shrugged. Jonah didn't want to be mothered around.

He looked so uncool. Tomorrow, he'll wear something not so daggy, I thought. But the next day it was the same old overalls and hat. We couldn't figure him out. He was like one of those blanks in Scrabble. But somehow, I wanted him to like us.

Jonah got picked on, especially by Watts and Tommo. They thought everything about him was dumb. He mostly ignored them, which made them worse.

"Hey, derr brain, what do you wear that dumb hat for?" goes Watts.

"It looks real derr dumb dork," goes Tommo.

Jonah looked at Watts's baseball cap.

"Where's Chicago, then?"

"America," says Watts.

"Where?"

"I dunno."

Jonah looked at him without blinking. "It's better than wearing a dumb hat from some city and you don't even know where it is." Then he walked off.

"What are ya, a man or a mouse?" yells Tommo.

"Hey, mousie!" yells Watts. "Here's some cheesy cheesy cheese for ya," and he threw an empty Coke can at him.

"Why don't you flatten him?" said Mitch.

"Waste of time," said Jonah.

‽‽‽‽‽‽

In math we were doing prime numbers, and I was thinking if Jonah was a number, he'd be a prime number for sure. Something like 97 that you couldn't divide anything else into. Now, Wormz, he'd be a number everything could be divided into. He'd be easygoing number 12. Me, I take the simple way, I'm 10. Mitch is definitely number 1.

‽‽‽‽‽‽

We were sitting on the footpath after school, waiting for Nicko's mum to pick us up.

"What do you think of Jonah the Loner?" goes Mitch.

"I dunno. He doesn't say much," said Azza.

Mitch picked at the sole of his shoe. "He's weird."

"He's okay," said Nicko, "but we'll have to teach him a lot of things."

"Yeah," said Azza. "Can you believe he doesn't know how to

play rugby or basketball? Can you believe that?"

"He's been in a time warp," said Nicko. "He was the only kid in grade six at his old school."

"He used to help his dad a lot," said Azza, bouncing a bald tennis ball in the gutter.

"He's not a Coconut," said Mitch.

"He's a tough nut from Tubbut," said Nicko.

"Do we want him hanging round us?" goes Mitch.

"Give him a chance," said Azza. "If he wants to muck around with us, that's cool."

Anyway, after a bit of an argument, we decided Jonah was okay, but weird.

4 TEACHERS AND PARENTS

Teachers are very important in this story. I'm an expert on teachers. I've had plenty of them. I have observed their behavior all day for five days a week, for four terms a year, for almost seven years.

Good teachers have a sense of humor, and they know how to control the class, otherwise someone like Faith Williamson yells, *"Shut up, everyone!"* all the time.

Some teachers think the perfect class is a room full of statues, but with good teachers you *do* things. For example, Mr. Robinson yells, "Who wants to train for rugby after school on Wednesday?" and we all do.

We had a fantastic art teacher, Miss Rose. We made so much great stuff in art, our kitchen looked like a gallery. We'd carry all the new masterpieces in the kitchen door.

"Make way! Make way! For the next exhibition!"

Then in fourth term, Miss Rose left.

"Where are the new masterpieces?" said Mum.

"Miss Rose left."

"So?"

"We're still doing what we started three weeks ago."

Good teachers are strong. Once we had Miss Cleare. She was one big migraine. Watts used to time how long until she took an aspirin. Good teachers do not have nervous breakdowns because the kids give them a hard time. They don't *have* a hard time.

Also, there is something a bit mad about the best ones. We had a teacher once, he was so in love with nature we had cocoons and bones and dead penguins in our room, and he took us to the zoo so we could see the newborn baby orang-outang—on *Saturday!!!!!!!!*

These are the teachers going to camp with us:

MR. HOLMES He teaches 5/6H.

Mr. Holmes is a permanently crumpled person. I remember once he nearly hung himself on his tie. His car door slammed just as a gust of wind blew his tie, and he went to dash off because he was late and throttled himself. He always wears a tie. Maybe he thinks it looks professional. Anyway, it's always covered with stains. He is a nice person and he tries hard but he's HOPeLEsS!!!

"He's a nerd."

"No," says Mum, "nerd's the wrong word, too modern; he's a duffer."

MISS CAPPELLI We always say it in one word, like mischief. Antonia Cappelli. She teaches our class, 5/6C.

I'm in love with her. We're all in love with her. We're all going to marry her. She has a great smile, great teeth, great eyes, great personality, and a great sense of humor. Her legs are a bit short, but you can't have everything.

When she needs to, she has a voice that cuts through steel, and she can also do that whistle where you put your fingers in your mouth, which is good for taxis, but *earsplitting!!!!!!*

In class, without looking up, she goes, "Jason, if you're doing what I think you're doing, stop it *right now!*"

"What?" goes Jason.

"Cutting your eraser into tiny pieces and flicking them at Beth and Jessica up in the front."

Which is exactly what Jason is doing!

MRS. McDONALD She teaches 3/4M.

Mrs. Elizabeth McDonald. Grownups call her Betty or Bet. We call her Chook because she clucks around the place, scratching here, scratching there, like a chicken. If something goes right, she says, "Jolly beaut!" and if something goes wrong, she goes, "Blinking heck!" For something amazing, she says, "By jingo!" She wears Daisy Duck shoes.

Once, when some of the kids were giving her heaps, she yelled, "You can all go to billy-o, I don't care!" and she steamed out the door. Then she steamed back in again. "You *can't* go to billy-o, I *do* care!"

When my brother Adrian got her for a teacher last year, he had a real spaz attack.

"I don't want her. She teaches the vegetables!"

"Well, she's teaching you, cabbage head."

But at the end of the year he really liked her, and Mum said she was an excellent teacher.

MISS RIDDLE Lisa Riddle. She teaches art and Italian. We call her Lisa.

She's cool. She has thick black hair, which she twists around in different knots, and she wears floppy black clothes, big junk jewels, and funny-colored lipsticks. She goes to the park near school at lunchtime for a smoke. My uncle would call Miss Cappelli a babe, but he wouldn't call Lisa a babe.

She's good at accents (of course she's perfect at Italian), and she is the *best* at reading stories because she gives everybody the right voice. You should hear her. She could be on the *Late Show* or on the radio.

She also says things like, "Michael, have you got brains?"

"Yes," goes Wormz.

"Well, turn them *on!*"

"And Fawkner, where are your listening skills?" which she says in a cool, throaty way, but we know she means business.

Chook, Miss Cappelli, and Lisa were pleased about camp because they're all good friends. In summer, they go over to the park together and have their lunch sitting under the big trees. We see them laughing.

So now you know what the teachers are like.

There are also parents going to camp. The law says you have to have quite a few adults. For fifty-one kids we had to have six adults.

MRS. PUMMVITALEILLE, which is a name nobody knows how to say. We call her Mrs. Pumps-Vital. She's Pascal's mum.

She talks and talks. We also call her No Gaps. If there's a hole in the conversation, she feels really uncomfortable. She's okay. Just.

MR. MURPHY Jessica's dad.

He's good. Actually, thinking about him, I would say he is a gentleman...like, a gentle man. He always tries to help. If Mr. Murphy asks you to do something, you do it because it would be rude not to. He never yells.

One evening, we wanted to go on the trampoline and none of the teachers would supervise. They said they needed a break. Mr. Murphy took his coffee to the tramp and missed out on all the juicy teacher-talk. Little Tak, a mad Trekkie, sat beside him and told him the whole plot of *Deep Space 9*. Mr. Murphy, who's never seen *Star Trek*, listened carefully.

If you ask Mr. Murphy something, he always thinks and then replies. Sometimes it's a drag because you have to listen to a long answer. He's the opposite of Mrs. Pumps-Vital. Mum was pleased when she heard Mr. Murphy was going to camp. She says he has a calming influence.

So now you know what the parents are like. If you're wondering about the wombat, it comes later.

5 THE BOMB

Introducing MR. BRIAN CROMWELL, otherwise known as Crom the Bomb, or simply The Bomb.

He was sent to our school from another school, where I bet they had a massive "The Bomb's Gone Off!!!!" party when he left.

None of the parents like him, and at the end of the year the principal had a line of parents who announced loudly, "Whatever happens, I do not want my child in Mr. Cromwell's class next year."

Mr. Cromwell became a teacher so he could be bossy and mean. He should have gone into the army. Occasionally, he is okay. I heard he was nice for a day back in 1876.

I was in his class last year. He has a funny walk, and he's a sneaky bottle-basher, a grog artist. He thinks nobody knows he drinks, but everybody does.

They put Cromwell teaching the grade fours. They wouldn't dare give him the tender little kindergartners. It would be cruelty to dumb animals. Besides, kindergarten mothers are like mother bears, and they would tear him down with their claws and rip him to shreds. If he had grade six it would be open warfare, and kids would bring bazookas to school, so they buried him in the middle with poor old grade four. A couple of kids left our school rather than be in The Bomb's class.

The parents were furious.

"Why don't they fire him?" said Jude from next door.

Mum was mending my jeans. "You can't just fire a teacher. It's a great rigmarole: letters of complaint, days to respond, support groups, counseling, the whole catastrophe. Besides, we can't prove he's done anything wrong."

"Why does he keep teaching?"

"Well, frankly," said Mum with a sigh, trying to undo a knot in the thread, "I think he enjoys it."

This year my brother lost the lottery. He got put in The Bomb's class. Even he didn't deserve that. At least he was with his best mate, Max.

"I'm sorry, Adrian," said Mum. "Let's just see how we go. It's only for a year."

ONLY for a *YEAR!* What does she think that is? Two days? A year is forever!

Mum went on. "Remember how you didn't want to be in Mrs. McDonald's, and it turned out fine? Well, you never know, this year might turn out fine, too."

"Yeah," I added. "The Bomb might get struck by lightning. Be thankful, Adrian," I said with brotherly concern. "Just be glad he's not your dentist."

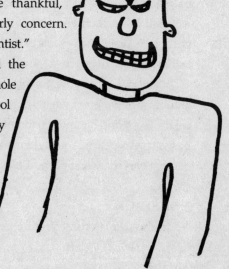

You know something, all the teachers, the principal, the whole "school community," the school council, and a tribe of angry parents couldn't shift The Bomb...but Jonah did.

6 How to Be Unpopular in Five Easy Lessons, the Brian Cromwell Way

1. GO OFF LIKE A BOMB

You think you're doing the right thing, then suddenly he goes psycho at you. *Detention!*

2. BE MEAN

Once on a school outing, after twenty minutes on the bus, Phillip, this little kid, says, "I want to go to the toilet."

Well, The Bomb didn't remind us about going before we got on the bus. Us big kids could hang on, but this little kid sat hunched up with his skinny legs crossed and twisted round, looking miserable and pathetic. We all knew how he felt.

Faith Williamson and Kristelle went up and said, "Mr. Cromwell, Phillip really badly wants to go to the toilet." Cromwell told them to mind their own business. Would he stop the bus? NO WAY!!!!!

Phillip wasn't making any noise, but he had tears in his eyes, and his legs were red where they pressed together so hard. And we drove on and on and on and on for kilometers, and the whole bus was whispering. You can guess what happened in the end. I bet that was the worst day in Phillip's life.

3. BE SLACK

In the whole of last year he gave us two projects. We had to have them in exactly on time. A couple of kids were late. *Detention!* But he didn't look at those projects for ages and ages.

"When are we getting our projects back, Mr. Cromwell?" asks Faith Williamson.

"Never!" whispers someone in the back. *Detention!*

So unfair. Kids in other classes got hologram stickers saying "Fabulous," "Far out," "Neat," and their teachers wrote nice stuff about what they'd done. But we'd get our projects back about two months later with one word, like "Fair." We didn't even try to do good work. What was the point?

4. DO SLOW TALK

The Bomb loves to hear his own voice. When he gets mad, he talks slowly, letting the words drip out one by one: "I   suppose you   think   it   doesn't   matter   if   the   toilets   look like   a   swamp," and he rocks backward and forward on his heels. Then he hurls the thunderbolt. *Detention!*

Once, after a magnificent performance of slow talk, when he took about an hour to say thirty words, the whole class plotted together, and we wrote our homework   all

spaced   out

like   this

Guess what happened. Starts with the letter D. But he got the message, because he didn't do any slow talk for a couple of weeks after that. (Beth the Good did her homework properly, and she got detention, too! Probably for being such a goody-goody!)

D x 28 = us

5. GIVE DETENTIONS

Besides the D-word, The Bomb has an arsenal of mean tricks up his sleeve. If you rock back on your chair, he makes you kneel at your desk, and that hurts so badly.

HO NO
A SPECK!

If you leave a crumb after eating lunch, you have to clean up the whole school ground.

If you're not paying attention, he does his ruler trick, e.g.: Matos is asleep in the back; The Bomb creeps up beside him, takes Matos's ruler, and smashes it down on the table, right by his ear; Matos leaps out of his skin; the ruler is toothpicks.

On the first day of school, I said to Adrian, "I dare you to ask The Bomb the meaning of tire ant." My brother got the first detention of the year. For impertinence. Look it up.

And it was all quadruply unfair because I had the best teacher in the Southern Hemisphere, the gorgeous Miss Cappelli.

But camp was going to be a totally Bomb-free zone!

7 JONAH RIDES TO SCHOOL

Starting from his first morning, Jonah rode his bike to school. So what? Well, you're not allowed to ride your bike to our school because the school council thinks it's too dangerous. So the principal, Mrs. Furgus, sent Jonah home with a note saying, "Don't let your child ride a bike to school."

Next morning, Jonah and his dad rode bikes to school, and they arrived just as Mrs. Furgus climbed out of her car.

"Could I have a word with you, please?" said Jonah's dad in a fairly loud voice.

"Certainly," said Mrs. Furgus. "Would you like to come into my office?"

"No thanks," said Jonah's dad. "Here's fine. My son is going to ride his bike to school."

"No," said Mrs Furgus. "The school council policy committee formulated the policy, approved by the school council, that forbids the riding of bikes to our school."

"Now you listen to me," said Jonah's dad. "My boy can come to school by elephant or submarine if we want him to. As long as there's no hassle for school staff and he's not on school property, it's none of your business."

"No," said Mrs Furgus. "It's too dangerous for our children to ride to school."

Jonah's dad took a deep breath and went to scratch his head

in frustration but found he had his bike helmet on. A crowd had gathered around because the voices were raised, and it was all pretty interesting.

"Now, you obviously see it differently," said Jonah's dad, "but this is the way I see it. If you want your kid to go in the water, you teach him to swim, right? If you want your kid to ride a horse, you teach him to ride. If you want your kid to get around the city, you teach him to catch a tram or walk or ride a bike. Now, I know it's not like out in the sticks, but the only way your kid's going to learn how to get around the streets is to teach him to get around the streets, and let him get on with it."

Mr. Theodoridis, one of the school council, stepped forward (which annoyed Mrs. Furgus, because she can look after herself). Mr. Theodoridis can't keep his mouth shut.

"It's too dangerous."

Jonah's dad sighed. "Do you think I'm trying to kill my boy? Maybe the fumes have affected your brain."

"We want what's best for our children," piped up a mum on Mrs. Furgus's side.

"Fair enough. Well, how about giving them some fresh air?" said Jonah's dad. "And if not, how about you get yourself another planet, and leave this one for the people who *like* fresh air?"

Meanwhile, Jonah had chained his bike up to a gum tree with a heavy motorbike chain.

Jonah's dad turned around to the assembled crowd. "Why don't you teach your kids how to live instead of stuffing them in the back seat of a car all the time? Poor little mollycoddled mites."

He swung himself onto his bike and, as an afterthought,

yelled, "I'll weld you a bike rack any time you change your mind," and rode off.

So now you know what Jonah's dad's like.

Boy, oh boy, oh boy, oh boy!!! Nobody had *ever* spoken to Mrs. Furgus or Mr. Theodoridis like that.

There was Jonah, son of his rude, offensive dad, standing with his bike helmet in his hand. Were they going to beat him to death with cricket bats from the sports locker?

Mr. Theodoridis was a violent red in the face, muttering about agenda and policy committee and school council, reviewed, voted, etc., etc., etc.

After that, Jonah rode his bike to school every morning and chained it up to a tree in the street where the teachers park their cars.

LOATHE AT FIRST SIGHT

"The Bomb's going to collect some medicine from Auntie Boozer," we said at lunch when we saw him drive off in his collection of dints and scratches.

We were sitting on the wall of the big kids' playground when he returned. He drove very slowly up over the edge of the concrete curb by the tree where Jonah's bike was chained. Then his car flopped back down and stopped just as he crunched one side of the bumper on the sidewalk.

The Bomb climbed out and looked at his car and how it was parked. Then he noticed a scratch along the side of his car. Then he looked at the pedal of Jonah's bike. Then he looked at us.

Jonah did the worst thing he could possibly have done. He grinned.

Cromwell slowly smiled as he walked toward us. "Yes, funny isn't it?" When The Bomb smiles, you think of an animal baring its teeth.

"Stay behind after school and share the little joke!" he said to Jonah.

There was no car paint on Jonah's bike pedal.

From then on, at every opportunity, The Bomb picked on Jonah like he was a scab on his knee. Lucky Jonah wasn't in his class!

Ever since I told Mum about Jonah's dad and the bikes, she was always asking about him, like she was doing research into him or something. "How's Jonah?" she'd ask.

We were playing Spit.

"He's okay," said Wormz. "I don't think he's had much practice at making friends. You know how some kids offer you candy? Well, Jonah offers facts. At the library, he gets out information books on camels or bog bodies, that sort of stuff, especially about animals."

"He gets *Australian Geographic* in the mail," said Nicko. "And he says Tubbut, where he comes from, is a palindrome, which is a word that's the same backward, and there are seven palindrome town names in Australia."

"Hey, I'm a living palindrome!" said Azza.

"How about the frog fact?" said Wormz. "He reckons there's a frog that hatches its babies through its mouth."

"He says the human body gives off a hundred watts of heat, and that's when you're sitting down," said Azza.

"He doesn't fit in," said Mitch.

"Yes, he does," said Azza.

"No, he doesn't," said Mitch.

"Sometimes he doesn't have an expression on his face," said Nicko. "He makes some people annoyed just by the look of him. He looks too dead serious, which makes you think he's putting it on. Some people think it's cheeky." Nicko thought for a moment. "Actually, he's a hard person to be friends with because he doesn't really, sort of, join in."

"Yoo-hoo!" That was Jude. She's a real character. Jude and Bruno live next door. Jude's always in our place. She and Mum play basketball on a team called the Cellulites. They sat down with a cup of coffee.

"He's an unusual kid," said Mum. "An only child." (Guess who they're talking about!)

"Funny, isn't it," said Jude. "Farming families...You expect them to have lots of kids, breed like rabbits, you know, fresh air, good food and all that."

THE BOMB VS. JONAH: ROUND 2

Adults won't find this bit very tasteful. Sorry, it can't be helped, it's what happened.

Every Friday morning we have assembly. The whole school goes to the church hall next door and sits on bits of old carpet, the kindergartners down front and the big kids in the back. Each assembly, one class does some items, like sings some songs or acts a play.

This was The Bomb's assembly, and his class was standing up front in three rows ready to spout this boring poem that he'd chosen. All the little kindergartners and grade ones down in the front were wriggling, squeaking, and picking threads out of the edge of the old carpet.

The Bomb waited for silence. He turned on the Glare. His eyebrows join up in the middle, his left eyebrow goes up at the end, then he pulls his chin back in, and his eyes burn like a laser. It's impossible to look at him. Mitch looked at him for three seconds once and nearly died.

Everyone shushed quickly, because even the little kiddies could see this was not a man to annoy.

He gave an extra three seconds of Glare to make the silence last.

T o t a l   q u i e t .

Then he turns to his class and bends down to pick up his poetry book from the floor. As he bends down with his backside pointing toward the audience, there is the *loudest fart* I have *ever heard!!*

"Pardon me," says Jonah clearly, in an absolutely flat voice.

Honestly!!!!!!!!!!!!!! In front of 237 children, 13 staff, 42 mums and dads, and the lunch ladies! Everyone nearly *died.* The adults tried not to crack up. Mrs. Furgus immediately stood and firmly told everyone to settle down, and muttered something to Jonah.

The Bomb would have killed him right then, but there were so many witnesses he had to go on with the show.

The poem was about the pioneers; full of rhymes like "toil" and "soil," "star" and "afar." Each kid recited two lines. It was going okay until Sarah Johnson, who has a loud nasal voice, did her bit: "…and the wild bees gum from the knotted hum…"

Plus, the whole school was giggling and wriggling in memory of the fart. The Bomb was ready to deep-fry everybody in boiling oil. He wanted to give the whole school detention for the rest of the year. But the principal got up and ranted about disgusting behavior, setting an example, rudeness, etc., etc.

Jonah sat there with a serious face, as if he was agreeing with everything she said. It was the best assembly.

"Hey, Jonah, was that a real fart or a fake?" said Nicko.

"You were sitting next to him!" said Wormz. "Did you need a gas mask?"

Maybe it was real. Jonah wasn't telling, but it was 100% convincing, and the timing was perfect. Jonah became a legend.

Needless to say, The Bomb's hatred of Jonah heated up to the boiling point. He only had to pass him in the corridor and he would find Jonah doing something wrong.

He'd squash Jonah like he was a beetle, then he'd lift his foot to see if he was dead. The beetle would be still for a moment, then he'd start running again. Then The Bomb would squash him harder, but he'd still keep going. You know what I mean? You think, How can that beetle still be alive?

It upset other kids to see him picked on so much, but at least The Bomb wasn't picking on them. Jonah didn't fight back. He didn't seem to care.

?!?!!!

One Wednesday night, Mum came home from basketball and flopped down on the couch.

"We lost again," she said in a matter-of-fact voice. "We were faster," she stretched her arms above her head and yawned, "but they were bigger."

Then she sat up, alert. "But I found out something about your Mr. Cromwell."

"He's not mine, he's Adrian's."

"What, Mum? What?" goes Adrian.

"Well, a woman on the other team used to teach with him years ago. He was a gym teacher. She said he was keen on the outdoors stuff, rock climbing and canoeing, and a real ace at archery. He was a coach, a bachelor, liked a beer. She said he was bossy, but he was okay."

?!?!!!

"Quite interesting," said Nicko, "but ask your mum to get some juicier goss."

10 GETTING READY FOR CAMP

Camp was going to be so so so so cool!!!!!!!!! I made a quick trip to Safeway to stock up on tooth-rotters.

For camp you have to label everything. I said, "The only thing that's not labeled that's going to camp is me."

"With any luck you'll get lost," said my ugly brother Adrian.

Mum and me crammed all my camp stuff into our big black bag.

"Adrian, leave my Venus flytrap alone. And don't go forcing flies into its mouths, you'll give it indigestion. Mum, don't let him touch it."

Then Jude came in. She and Mum had a cup of coffee while I looked for my other thong.

Jude asked, "How's Jonah?"

Now both of them are doing research, I thought.

"Well, he says his jacket is made out of sixteen plastic drink bottles," I said.

"I've got some more on our Brian Cromwell," said Jude. (Now he's *our* Brian Cromwell!) Jude leaned forward. "It's actually quite shocking. He was teaching archery, and a kid shot an arrow into his foot! Can you imagine!"

"Oh, poor man. Wouldn't you just die!" said Mum.

"Did he kill the kid?" asked Adrian.

"No," I said, "but he's getting back at every kid ever since."

"*We* didn't arrow him in the foot," said Adrian.

"We would if we could," I said.

"Don't be silly," said Mum.

"Why didn't he give up teaching?" said Adrian.

"Like getting back on your horse after you've fallen off. Now we know why he walks funny," I said.

"That's not a strong enough reason for his behavior," said Jude. "There's got to be more to it than that."

JONAH LIGHTS A FIRE

Jonah arrived at school very early on a cold morning. There was nobody else around. He cleared a space, got some paper out of the trash can, some sticks from under the trees, and lit a fire.

The smoke blew over near the school and set off the smoke detector. Along came the fire brigade, red lights flashing, bells ringing, and the police with sirens wailing and guns on hips. We arrived as they were leaving. Once again, in the middle of a terrible fuss, there was Jonah standing with his mouth shut and his eyes open, taking it all in.

Then an inspector from the Department of Education and Mrs. Furgus spent ages with him in the office questioning him closely about his reasons for the fire and didn't quite believe him when he said "to get warm."

Jonah said that at his old school each family had a key to the door so no one ever had to wait outside in the cold.

2 THE BIG DAY: LITTLE TIPS TO MAKE YOUR DEPARTURE EASY

1. Kissing

Parents actually get very excited about the whole camp deal and tell you a million times how quiet it's going to be without you and how much they'll miss you. It's a good idea to get the kissing over before you leave home. You don't want your mother slobbering on you as you're climbing on the bus. That is *so* gross.

2. Hide the tooth-rotters

If your mother finds them, she'll say, "You aren't supposed to take candy to this camp. Besides, you can't *possibly* eat all those!" Put them in your boots. She won't look there.

3. Don't forgets

Get all the "don't forget"s at home, too. There will be heaps, especially about being clean, e.g.: *"Don't forget to clean your teeth!"*

Last camp, the same thing happened every night after Lights Out. Lying in bed, I'd suddenly remember, I forgot to clean my teeth!

Tim Oldfield, he's got a toothbrush and a tube of toothpaste that have been at nine school camps and never been used! Ever. It's a tradition in his family.

"And change your clothes occasionally!"

Last year, my ugly brother Adrian wore the same clothes all camp. Deciding which clothes to put on was too much for his tiny brain. Actually, I myself have been known to wear the same pair of socks for quite a while. And Kelly had her hair in the same ponytail for one whole camp.

kelly

3 SAND TIGER SHARKS

"Boy, oh boy, have I got news!" Azza raced up, bouncing a basketball, and he was bouncing, too. "My auntie Gina cleans houses in St. George's Road, Toorak, which is *really* posh, and you'll *never* guess who lives in one of the houses—The Bomb's *mum!*

"She's a bossy old stick named Iris Cromwell, and Gina says she dusts lots of photos of two other sons, Taylor and Elliot, but she doesn't dust any photos of Brian. She says Taylor is an executive in Ford America, and Elliot's a professor somewhere."

"How does she know it's really The Bomb's mum?" asked Mitch.

"Because Gina cleans the house three doors down, and the lady there told her about this other son who was a teacher at our school and everything, but they never talk about him because they had a big fight."

"Yay, team!" goes Wormz.

"You can't imagine The Bomb having a mother, can you?" said Nicko.

"And listen to this—Mother Bomb always inspects when Gina's finished cleaning, and gets her to do bits again that she's not happy with."

"Very familiar," said Mitch.

"What an old shark!" said Nicko.

Watts and Tommo were trying to get Jonah into trouble. On Monday morning, seats that had been freshly painted on Sunday were smeared with gravel, and the rumor got round the school that Jonah had done it to get back at the school for the fire thing. Some people wanted to believe it. It was all whisperings, but my ugly brother Adrian saw Watts and Tommo near the seats last thing on Sunday.

"Watts and Tommo are sharks, too," said Mitch.

"Sand tiger sharks," said Jonah. "The mother sand tiger has a lot of babies growing inside her, then the strongest babies eat their brothers and sisters before they're born."

"What do you mean?" said Nicko. "They eat their brothers and sisters *inside* their mother?"

"Yes. The two strongest survive."

"Eurgggghhh! Gross!" said Wormz. "You mean they actually eat their…Oh, yuck!…They're cannibals!"

14 THE BUS FOR CAMP WILL BE LEAVING PROMPTLY AT 8 O'CLOCK. PLEASE BE PUNCTUAL!

It was *so* funny last year. Adrian was charging round at four o'clock in the morning yelling, *"Come on! Hurry up! We'll be late for the bus!"* He had on his Mambo T-shirt, with his lunch in a paper bag and everything, *at four o'clock in the morning!* He woke up Jude and Bruno!

At 8:30, the bus is still there, and the engine has been going for fifteen minutes. Mr. Murphy, who is driving to camp in his car so that we have an emergency vehicle, left ten minutes ago. The bus driver is in a grump because Tommo, who was helping to pack the bags, threw a heavy pack onto the driver's bag, which had his thermos in it, and Mitch's luggage is too heavy to lift.

The bus is crawling with excited kids. Azza is bouncing a little superball off everything, including Lily's head. Kids wave down from the windows, parents wave up. Wormz is doing a handstand on his seat, waving good-bye to his parents with his feet.

"Hey, Wormz, your parents have gone!"

"I can still wave good-bye to them."

From high up in the bus, I can see Nicko's little sister ripping buds off a daisy bush, but Mrs. Nicko is chatting so hard she doesn't notice.

Renee is flapping around screaming, "I've totally lost my teddy!"

"Don't catastrophize!" goes Miss Cappelli. "Look for him! I bet I'm hoarse when we get back!" she says to Lisa.

Mrs. Somerville is wearing dark glasses. Her dear little Lukie Pukie is going so very very far far away all by himselfie-welfie.

Parents are making signals, miming last instructions, blowing kisses, and looking deliriously happy.

"I'll miss you, darling!" yells Mrs. Mitch to Mitch, then she turns to Mrs. Powell and says, "Won't it be lovely to have a bit of peace and quiet?"

"Bliss!" says Mrs. Powell.

"All those who get sick, sit up front!" yells Chook.

"Stow your small bags above your head," yells Miss Cappelli.

Mr. Holmes counts us for the sixteenth time. He's still wrong.

Suddenly, the driver swings into his seat and reaches for the lever. With a *chee-ooooooooof*, the bus door folds shut. There's a flap of pink hands.

Goodbyegoodbyegoodbyegoodbyegoodbyegoodbye…

We're off at last!!!!!!!!!!!!!!

"It begins when the bus wheels start rolling," says Nicko.

"It begins when the bus driver shuts the door," says Azza.

"I reckon it begins when you put your foot on the ground from the bus when you get there," says Mitch.

"It's begun," says Jonah as we pass The Bomb's car.

"Want a lolly?" says Wormz.

We look out of the bus window and we're passing people in the street who are having an ordinary day.

44

15 ARE WE THERE YET? ARE WE THERE YET? ARE WE THERE YET?

Chook said it was a long drive. She said when we got to the steep hills called the Black Spur we would be nearly there. We pulled up at the first traffic lights near a massive red and gold Chinese restaurant.

"Is that Gumbinya Pioneer Camp?" goes Wormz.

We sat at the back of the bus and sang:

"Everybody knows that we are the best
We're gonna put you to the test
So fasten your seat belts, step on the gas
We're gonna kick you in the...everybody
We will, we will rock you, drop you, pick you up and sock you
We will, we will r-o-c-k you."

Matos sang out, "Rubber ducky, you're the one..."

"Hail to the bus driver, bus driver, bus driver man."

We stopped at a red light beside a bus of old people on an outing. We were yelling and singing, and they were sitting like zombies and didn't want to know about us, except one little old lady who waved and smiled and blew us kisses.

"I bet they won't have as much fun where they're going!" said Nicko.

45

Kristelle sings, *"Can you feel the love tonight…?"*

"No, I can't!" yells Mitch.

"Miss Lucy had a steamboat, the steamboat had a bell
Miss Lucy went to heaven and the steamboat went to
Hello operator, give me number nine
And if you disconnect me I will cut off your
Behind the 'frigerator, there was a piece of glass
Miss Lucy sat upon it and she broke her little
Ask me no more questions, tell me no more lies
The boys are in the bathroom, pulling down their
Flies are in the kitchen, bees are in the park
The boys and girls are kissing in the
d-a-r-k, d-a-r-k, d-a-r-k, dark, dark, dark."

Beth the Good had a nosebleed. Mrs. Pumps-Vital told Chook all about her renovations. Lukie Pukie told Mr. Murphy all about his new flashlight, his new sleeping bag, his new slippers, his new toothbrush, and his new bar of soap.

"We wanna we wanna we wanna wee.
If you don't stop for us, we'll do it on the bus."

We stopped halfway and ate our paper-bag lunch from home.

By the time we got to the Black Spur, we were expecting mountains like the Himalayas. The bus wound up the road through the forest. It rolled around the corners like a boat in a rough swell.

We swayed, "WHOOOOOOOOOOOOOO!!!!"
"WHAAAAAAAAAAAAAAAAAAAAAAAAAAAAAAAA!!!!!!!"
"WHOOOOOOOOOOOOOOOOOOOOOOO!!!"
"WHAAAAAAAAAAAAAAAAAAAAAAAAAA!!!"

We were getting close. There were signs like this:

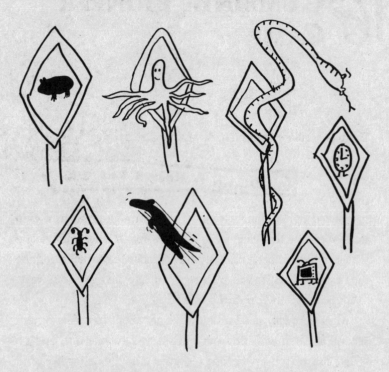

Mitch kept asking Rebecca, DoubleDeckerBeckerBus, "Are you sick yet?"

"I'll come right up close and tell you when I am," said BeckerBus.

Sean was white as a ghost, looking miserable, clutching his sick bag.

Chook handed out barley sugars to the pale faces, and suddenly there were twenty people feeling sick, including us in the back, and we were still singing our heads off.

"Get away with you," goes Chook.

16 GUMBINYA PIONEER CAMP

The bus lumbered off the highway at a sign saying:

Gumbinya Pioneer CAMP 2 K

It growled uphill along a country road through an arch of gum trees. We came to a gateway in an old wooden fence with wagon wheels and total bush on both sides. Branches scraped along the top of the bus, which was pretty exciting. We did a Mexican wave. *"Yeah, yeah, yeah! We're nearly there!"*

Miss Cappelli yelled a quick riot act about representing our school, and remembering our pleases and thank-yous, and no scrunching up toilet paper and flicking it onto the ceiling like what happened at the last camp.

Roosters and chooks squawked away as the bus rolled into the middle of a massive collection of old stuff: buildings and carts and wagons and everything old you can think of, including a wagon with solid wooden wheels like something from *The Flintstones*.

The bus door folded open and there was a lady about Mum's age. She had Doc Martens on her feet and a tatty old blue skirt down to the ground, plus a gray blouse and a dirty, worn apron. Her hair was roughly scrunched on top of her head, but a lot of it was straggling round her brown wrinkled face. She definitely looked like a pioneer. Her arms and her hands looked like a man's. Behind her was a little black dog.

"Hop down from the bus." She had a nice gravelly Australian voice. We all scraggled out and sat down under a huge gum tree.

"I'm Mary." She waved away a fly. You could tell by her eyes she liked the look of us. And we liked the look of her.

"Welcome to Gumbinya. We live like the pioneers here. No great comfort, but a lot of fun."

Kylie, who's probably never even done a wee behind a tree, looked very worried. "You'll be fine," goes Mary with a smile. "We'll have a great time."

Then round the corner stroll these two funny-looking people, talking and laughing. There was a huge bloke in a ripped yellow T-shirt and purple overalls, with a round chubby face and a crew cut, and a little lady with straight hair, Mambo shirt, tight pink bike shorts, and a stud in her nose.

"This is Helmut and Edwina."

None of us had ever seen a Helmut or an Edwina before. This was going to be so cool.

"Helmut's from Germany and Edwina's from England. They're traveling round the world, and luckily for me, they've stopped here for a while."

Matos, who was sitting near Helmut, asked, "Are you a giant?" Helmut bent down, grabbed him round the waist, and held him upside down.

"What was the question again?" goes Helmut.

Suddenly: "Aeeeeeeeeh! OOhhhhh! Yeeeaaaaaaaaah!" Wild screeches from the kids at the back. "A baby *wombat!*"

Mary sighed. "I might have known."

"Oh, he's so *cute!* He's a little block of fur with a leg on each corner."

"Look at his divine little nose."

"Oh, isn't he *cute?* He is *so* cute!"

"*QUIET!*" yelled Laserlungs Cappelli. *"Listen to Mary!!!!!!!!!!"*

"That's Bulldozer come out to meet you." Mary was serious. "Now, kids, please don't pat him. I know it's the hardest thing in the world, but it's for his own good. He's a wild animal, and when he's older he's going back to the bush."

Bulldozer snuffled around us. Jonah was grinning from ear to ear. Our hands hovered over Bulldozer's back, but no one touched him.

"Besides being a camp for you kids," said Mary, "this is also an animal refuge. People bring injured animals to me. I'll tell you Bulldozer's story later.

"Now a word about candy." (Wormz's pockets were so full of it his shorts were falling down!) "We asked you not to bring candy because of the animals. Also, there's a wombat here called Thornton Primary. He's the one to watch out for. He's older, bigger, and stronger than Bulldozer. Just leave him alone."

"And ants!" added Edwina. "In the last school, a little laddie had a private sweet feast in his sleeping bag after Lights Out. Next morning, he woke up with his pillow and sleeping bag and everything absolutely crawling with ants in his sticky lolly dribble."

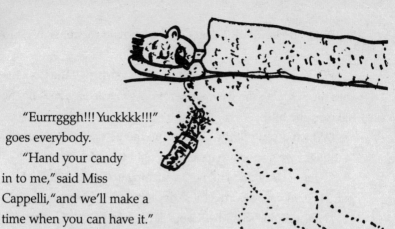

"Eurrrgggh!!! Yuckkkk!!!"
goes everybody.

"Hand your candy
in to me," said Miss
Cappelli, "and we'll make a
time when you can have it."

"One last thing," said Mary. "There
are animals, tree stumps, tent ropes, and
pegs around, so please don't run. You can play rugby
in that paddock." We looked at the paddock. Two dopey donkeys
stood at the fence and stared back.

"When you hear the ship's bell, everybody back here under
the tree, pronto. Now unpack and get yourselves settled in."

We had already been divided into tent and duty groups. There
were Squatters, Miners, Bushies, Swaggies, Settlers, Troopers,
Drovers, Selectors, Explorers, and Convicts. We were the Convicts:
Wormz, Azza, Nicko, Jonah, Mitch, and me. Naturally, the
Convicts were the best.

Thanks to nifty footwork by Nicko, a near disaster was
avoided. When we first got off the bus, Nicko was busting, so he
dashed for the toilet, a colonial wooden building with
twentieth-century plumbing. As he was coming out, he saw Mr.
Holmes hanging little signs on the tents...Convicts, Settlers,
Drovers, etc.

Nicko sneaked around to find the Convicts. HORROR!!!

HORROR!!! HORROR!!! The Convicts were in the tent closest to the teachers!

Without Mr. Holmes seeing him, Nicko switched the Convicts with the Settlers, who were farthest from the teachers, back up the hill near the bush.

"Why did you put the Convicts up there?" said Miss Cappelli. "I thought we decided to have them right under our noses?"

"I dunno," said Mr. Holmes, scratching his leg. "I thought I did put…I could have sworn…Must have made a mistake. Sorry."

"Never mind," said Miss Cappelli. "It might be best in the long run."

The teachers were in a comfy country cabin, which had an open fire, a lounge, and a snazzo new kitchen.

"Miss Cappelli, you're not pioneers! You've got a fridge, a microwave, and a TV!" said Wormz.

"We're the Future!" said Miss Cappelli. "Now, you beetle back to the pioneering days and leave us in peace."

So we pioneered our bags out of the bus and lugged them up the hill to our tatty old army tent on a raised-up wooden platform floor. It had been in the wars. It was ripped and patched.

Bliss! Happiness! Wombats! No homework! No Bomb!

Camp was like home for Jonah, not that he was jumping

round shouting it. His eyes were smiling, and his face was a big wide grin. For the first time, we saw him happy.

"Hey, guys, pioneer yourselves over here," goes Mitch, waving from the Explorers' tent. "Have a squiz at this."

The fearless Explorers were Rebecca, Sarah, Melissa, Alice, and Kristelle. Sarah is mad about Winkipinki. In case you don't know, Winkipinki is this little Japanese girl cat with a tartan dress and a tartan bow who says things like: "I wonder what to say when I meet the flowers," and "I just love days like this."

Sarah has a Winkipinki mug, towel, face cloth, slippers, lunch box, pencil, eraser, notebook, and a zillion other things, which she arranged on her suitcase by her bunk. It looked like an altar in a church for Saint Winkipinki.

"Hey, Mitch!" goes Wormz. "Imagine Sarah on an exploring trek through the bush. Winkipinki is saying, 'Hello, pretty bush. I love starving to death in you.'"

"Hello, pretty snake," goes Mitch, "enjoy your breakfast of my foot."

"Hello, redback spider. Will you be my friend?" says Nicko.

?!?!?!

We swarmed all over the camp, checking it out. It was obvious that, if you lived around here, when something conked out or grew old but still might come in handy, you gave it to Mary.

Nothing was new. The big rec hall was a graveyard of bashed-up couches. In the bathrooms, all the taps were different, and there was a patchwork of tiles in the showers. We counted twenty-three different sorts of kitchen chairs in the dining room.

The showers were very pioneering, with the odd cockroach and spider. The thingie that the water squirts out of was high up,

way over your head, and most of the squirts missed you completely and squirted the wall.

Wormz and I followed a little track past the blacksmith's and through the bush. We came down to a river. Some kids were there, and a wombat eating grass. Watts flicked Thornton Primary's ear with a stick.

"Leave him alone," said Jonah. "You're bothering him."

"Who gives?" said Watts.

"If you pester him, he'll get to hate humans," said Jonah.

Tommo whacked Jonah hard on the back.

"March fly!" goes Tommo with a grin.

Jonah just looked at him, straight, until Tommo looked away.

17 BULLDOZER'S STORY

Mary took us on a tour of the old buildings, carts, and wagons. Her dog, Little Petal, and a black sheep called Mintie followed us. She told us about the pioneers, but she was having a hard time because Bulldozer got in between her legs and nearly tripped her up.

"Right-o," she said. "It's time to feed Bulldozer." She picked up the little wombat and sat on a stump. We sat in a huge ring around her.

"When I got him, he was as big and as bald as my thumb. I'll show you a baby wombat later, then you can see for yourself." (We saw it, in a bottle of preservative. It was tiny and naked and looked more like a witchetty grub than a wombat.)

"Bulldozer's mother was hit by a car on the road, but the farmer who knocked her knew that a tiny baby wombat can live inside its dead mother for up to three days. So he found little Bulldozer and brought him to me.

"Bulldozer sleeps in an old hat, where it's dark and comfortable and feels like his mum or a wombat hole, so he knows what it's like to be a wombat. If we don't pat him, and make a fuss of him, then he won't seek so much attention."

Edwina brought a bucket with a bottle in it.

"This is warm low-fat milk," said Mary. She put her arm around Bulldozer, like a baby, with his little feet sticking up, and she plugged in the bottle. He sucked immediately.

"Now, this bottle isn't like his mother, but it's the best I can do," said Mary.

You could see Bulldozer was drinking too fast. He pulled off the bottle, making a wheezing, rattling noise.

"Ever heard a wombat burp?" asked Mary. She patted him hard and rolled him. With every hard pat, or you could say soft smack, a cloud of dust rose up from the furry ball. Then he made a funny little milk-blurting sound. *Blup...blerrp!* But he kept rattling.

"We're not finished yet," said Mary. She rolled him and bumped him again. He nearly fell off her knee, but she hooked him back as if she'd done it a million times before.

Burrr...blupp! He wanted to drink again.

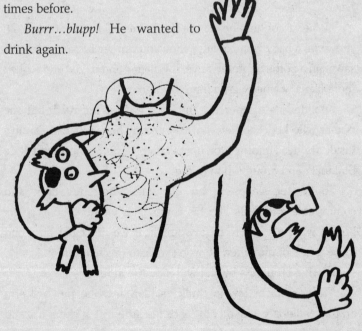

Mary sat on the stump, with Little Petal lying behind her, feeding and burping Bulldozer and answering our questions.

"How will you get him back to the bush?" asked Tak, which was my question, too.

"In the very early morning, when it's still dark, I take the wombats and the wallaby for a play, up in the bush. They snuffle around and have a lovely time.

"When they get older, like you kids, they change. They grow strong and become independent. They get the urge to go back to the bush. The wombats start to dig. They go looking for a mate. I'll take Bulldozer out for a little bit longer each night, until finally I'll leave him and he won't want to come home with me. Then I'll know my job is done."

We asked Mary dozens of questions, until she held up her hand. "Seeing as you're so interested, I'll show you a couple more of my patients."

In a scrumbly little nest in an old wardrobe there was a brush-tailed possum. We got a quick peep at a tiny sugar glider in a nesting box in a big aviary. Near Mary's house, we saw a young wallaby with one leg skinned to the bone where he'd been caught in a fence.

"Gee, Mary," said Mitch. "Add up the wild animals, the donkeys, chickens, horse, Mintie, Little Petal, and all us kids, and you've got a lot to look after!"

"You're not wrong!" said Mary.

18 MONDAY EVENING

Dinner was spaghetti and meatballs followed by banana pudding. My fork was like this, which is fine if you're trying to stab someone around a corner, but if you're trying to put food in your mouth, forget it.

Then we had to write in our Camp Journals. It was easy because there was so much to write about. Azza, as usual, got stuck. Remember how I said he was slow at some things? If Madonna bungee-jumped out of a helicopter into his backpack, he would still sit there, click-clicking his pen, trying to think of something to write about. He eats slow, too.

Mitch was smoking his pencil, lighting it with his eraser and writing as if he was signing big business deals.

Jonah did his journal in five seconds flat, full of things like what sort of pump Mary had on the dam, the hot water service, even the sort of phone Mary had.

Needless to say, Naomi ran out of space writing a prize-winning story about Mary being a world expert at getting wombats back to the bush.

I didn't care much about my journal. I was determined to take some fantastic photos to show Mum. My first film. Thirty-six photos. Thirty-six chances!

?!?!?

There weren't any lights to turn out, so Lights Out was all

flashlights. As usual, the teachers went into psycho-yelling overdrive, e.g.: *"Caleb, you've been running around with that towel around your waist clutching a toothbrush for half an hour. Just do it!"*

"Where's Nicko? Why isn't he in bed?"

"He's sitting on the toilet finishing his Garth Nix book."

"I can't find my teddy," whimpered Renee.

"Santa Cleopatra! Silènzio!" (That's Lisa.)

"Fawkner A. Mitchell, why aren't you in your pajamas? Do you have a death wish?" said Miss Cappelli.

"Haven't you heard, the children are the future?" said Mitch.

"You'll be the past in a minute! Get on with it."

The parents weren't as hard as the teachers. They hadn't done a university course in threatening. Mrs. Pumps-Vital said, "I'll tell Miss Cappelli and Mrs. McDonald if you don't be quiet." And Mr. Murphy had to listen to radiation particles, absolute zero, and hyper-acceleration warps trying to get Tak out of the bathroom.

The beds were squeaky wire bunks with mattresses covered with brown vinyl. When you moved, it sounded like you were rolling on a packet of cornflakes. My sleeping bag is made of nylon stuff, which is really slippery, and on that mattress it was like trying to sleep on an ice-skating rink.

Nicko's bunk sloped downhill. He found a board and stuck it under one end, trying to make it level.

The teachers threaten you for half an hour before you go to bed, then they threaten you for half an hour after, then they go into berserko overdrive for the next half hour and prowl like guards in a prison camp.

"Turn off that flashlight!"

LIGHTS OUT!

"*If I hear one more peep, you won't be Convicts, you'll be Astronauts!*"

"*Who was that giggling? Explorers, this is my last warning!*"

"*I didn't see a flashlight then, did I, Settlers?*"

We lay in the dark and talked quietly about Mary.

Mitch said, "Do you really believe she gets out of her warm comfy bed at four o'clock in the morning to take the animals to the bush? Do you reckon that's true?"

"For sure," said Nicko.

"I'll tell you about my uncle's dog," said Jonah quietly. "He was a young dog, kelpie–border collie cross. My uncle was training him with cattle.

"One evening, my uncle was looking for a lost cow when the dog got excited about a wombat hole. He raced down into it. My uncle could hear him barking and snapping down in the ground. He was making a tremendous din. He yelled and yelled to his dog to come out. Then the barking went strange and wild. Then it stopped." Jonah paused. "The wombat crushed the dog to death. Jammed him against the side of his burrow and broke his ribs."

We lay in the dark letting the story sink in. Nobody felt like talking anymore.

Then a couple of minutes later, Jonah added, "They're strong, wombats."

19 THE SECOND DAY

Jonah, who was already dressed, stuck his head in the tent. "The light was on all night in the bathroom of the teachers' hut."

"Didn't you go to bed last night?" groaned Nicko.

"Got up early. Mr. Holmes's got gastro. He's been chucking up all night. Mr. Murphy is taking him home and they're sending a replacement teacher."

"I'm sorry we're losing old Holmes Sweet Holmes," said Mitch. "You can get away with a lot with him."

But camp was so cool, we didn't think much about it.

At breakfast, they had humongous big plastic bottles of milk. I whooshed the milk into the plate and shot half my cornflakes out of the bowl. Edwina didn't get mad. She just said, "Clean it up, mate, and start again."

Watts was a garbage guts. For breakfast, he had nine Weetabix and four slices of toast and Vegemite, followed by three helpings of scrambled eggs and bacon. Worse than Wormz.

We Numbered Off to check how many kids had fallen down gold mines or died of snakebite. You have to yell your number **loud** and *fast,* and if Number Off gets stuck on you, you're in trouble. We have to go back to 1 again and waste time.

This is how we Numbered Off:

"1"

"2"

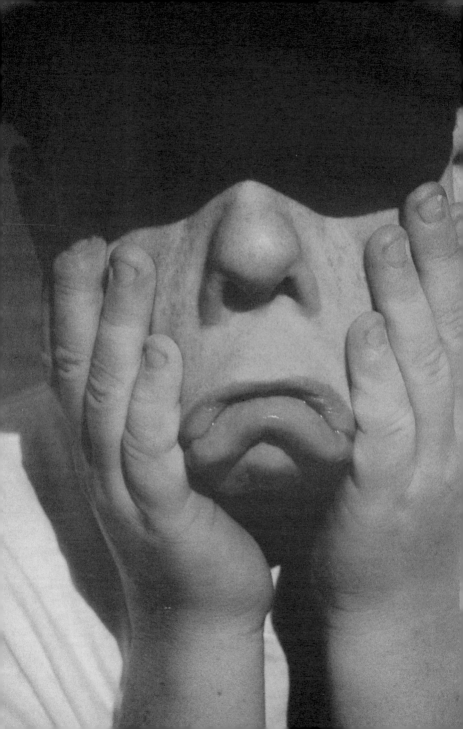

"Tree"

"4"

"5"

"Sex"

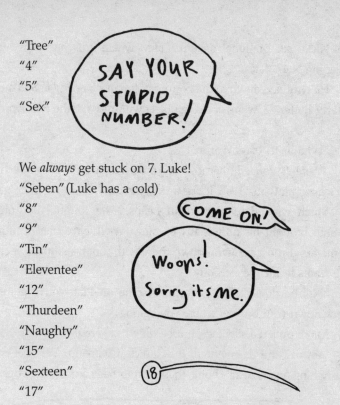

We *always* get stuck on 7. Luke!

"Seben" (Luke has a cold)

"8"

"9"

"Tin"

"Eleventee"

"12"

"Thurdeen"

"Naughty"

"15"

"Sexteen"

"17"

                      yells Sam from the boys' toilets

"19"

"TwenTEEEEEEEEEE!!!!!!!"

and so on.

Edwina timed us. The fastest time for Number Off was 49 seconds.

Then we had tent inspection to encourage neatness and tidiness. Unfortunately, I'm not neat, Mitch's housekeeper cleans his room, Wormz doesn't care, Nicko is hopeless, Azza was playing rugby, and Jonah was probably watching the wombats or talking to Mary.

Nicko sat on Jonah's bunk. "Hey, what's this bump in his sleeping bag?"

He wriggled down to the bottom of Jonah's bag and fished out a tatty, flattened, weird-looking object with most of the hair worn off.

"What is it?" says Wormz.

"Weren't you edumacated at kindermagarten?" goes Mitch. "It's a toy platypus. Well, it *was* a toy platypus."

Mitch wanted to give Jonah heaps. "The Tough Nut from Tubbut brought his little platty to camp. We'll leave him out for some air. It must be awful down there with Jonah's stinking feet. He wants to meet everybody."

"No, he doesn't," says Wormz. "Come on Plat, you're going back down your burrow where you belong."

Mitch pulled a silly face, but he didn't say anything more.

Wormz and I invented the Quick Clean-up. We stuffed everything under Azza's bunk, then put our bags around the edges

so you couldn't see the mess. But I won't recommend it, because our gear got so muddled up we couldn't find anything. Chook was suspicious and pulled one of the bags away, revealing all.

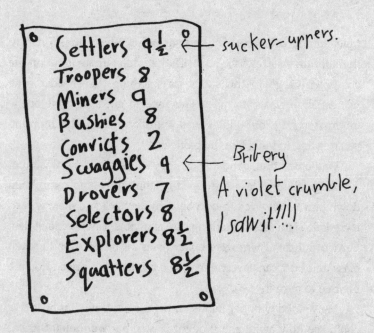

Settlers 4½ ← sucker-uppers.
Troopers 8
Miners 9
Bushies 8
Convicts 2
Swaggies 9 ← Bribery
Drovers 7   A violet crumble,
Selectors 8   I saw it!!!!
Explorers 8½
Squatters 8½

I was right. Jonah was sitting near Thornton Primary, watching him eat grass. Then a stack of girls came up. "Oh, he's *so* cute. He's so sweet. So a*dorable*!!!!"

"Don't feed him bread!"

"He likes it!"

"It's not good for him. He's a wild animal and he's going *back* to *the bush!*" Jonah yelled. He actually yelled!!!

20 WATTLE AND DAUB

Mary turned over a bucket and sat on it. "The pioneers had to think for themselves," she said. "They couldn't figure it out on the computer, or go to the shops for anything they needed. The nearest shop was sixty miles. They had to make do. One of the improvised ways of building was wattle and daub. This morning you're going to build like the pioneers."

Wattle was thin, bendable, whippy sticks, and daub was mud.

To get the wattle, we trooped up the hill behind camp, then down into a gully. We turned a bend in the track and there was an incredible sight like something out of a violent movie…a stolen, burned-out car! There were bullet holes in the door, and broken glass and beer cans everywhere. The robbers had ripped down a big tree to burn it.

Mary stood with her hands on her face, shaking her head. We could see how awful she thought it was, but we thought it was cool. Mitch pretended it was a prize in a TV show.

Jonah wasn't laughing. "A car got dumped near my uncle's. He had to drag it away because the place started looking like a junkyard."

¡¡!!¡¡

Back at camp, Mary showed us how to weave the sticks into a wall. "Then you make a mud mixture with straw to hold it together."

"Like mud bricks?" said BeckerBus.

IT'S A NEW CAR! The fabulous crash-track, totally ash model!!

The Wattlers

"Exactly," said Mary. "Then you slop it on the wall of sticks and smear it in."

Most kids were interested in the wattling, especially in using the tomahawk. Edwina had the wattlers. Helmut had the daubers. The Convicts volunteered to get the daub.

"I'll see you at the dam," said Helmut, "when I empty this wheelbarrow."

We stood on the bank of the dam, surveying the squooshy wallow of mud. Jonah scooped up a fistful.

"This is very fine mud," said Jonah, looking at it carefully. (Here we go, I thought, facts on mud.) "Wear it with pride!" Quick as a flash, he squooshed it down my face.

"Oh yes! Oh yes! Get the complete mud treatment!" goes Wormz. "Refresh the natural moisture balance of your skin!" He whacks a glob behind Mitch's knee. Mitch crumples against Azza, who steps back, slips, and slides on his bum into the mud hole.

Jonah sprang on him, slapping mud in his hair. "Deep revitalizing treatment for damaged follicles. It's gunky! It's gooey! It's squooshy, and it's yours for only five billion dollars, or free with every dual-flush toilet installed this weekend."

"Whaleman, you are improving!" says Mitch, slopping a juicy glob down Jonah's shorts.

"A combination of delicate oils and fragrances," goes Jonah, grabbing Mitch. "Deep" *sploosh* "revitalizing" *squish* "treatment" *squidge.* "This season's fragrance is dung!" *squelsh, squish, slosh, skrash!*

"Hey, Jonah! Slip! Slop! Slup!" goes Nicko, unloading both hands full.

"Your parents will abso*lute*ly lerv it!" says Jonah, getting him back.

Jonah was seriously funny. Maybe this was the real Jonah. Maybe this was why he liked us.

There was not a single millimeter of us that wasn't covered. We were weak with laughing. Wormz was a big grin of white teeth in a totally mud face.

Then we heard the *squeak, squeak* of the wheelbarrow.

"Helmut!"

"Will he freak out?" goes Nicko.

"I think he's cool, but you never know," says Mitch.

"What do we do?" goes Wormz.

"Act normal," goes Azza.

"Not possible!"

"Play dead!" says Jonah.

We dived down the bank of the dam and lay there like bodies in the First World War.

The squeaking stopped, then there was a mighty roar of laughter. "Oh, they're dead!" goes Helmut. "What a pity, I'd better bury them," and he started shoveling mud on us.

In between filling up the wheelbarrow, and mud sliding, and mud wrestling, we tried to catch those sneaky little crayfish yabbies with our bare hands.

Back at the wall, they were singing songs and swapping jobs, but nobody wanted to swap with the old daub diggers. We were like the drones down the mud mines in an outer galaxy. But we were having the best time! And Jonah wasn't following along with the fun, he was inventing it.

When it was time to finish, I got Helmut to take some photos. Then he pushed us in the dam.

"Not clean enough!" goes Helmut. "Aussie mud sticks hard."

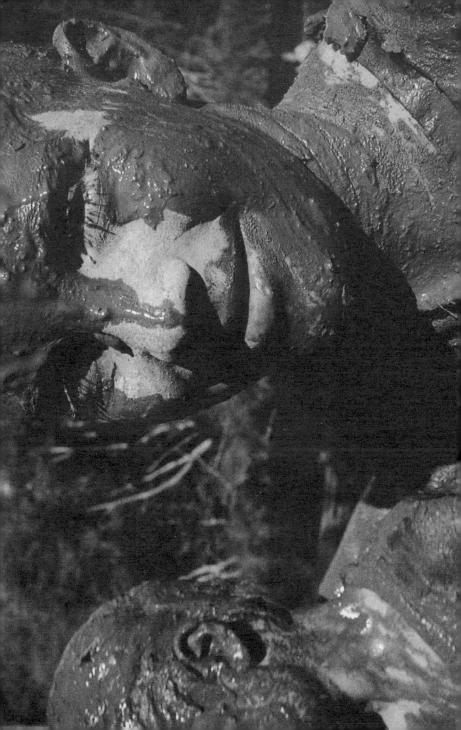

He kept pushing us back in. "And I have to clean the showers!"

It was nearly lunchtime. We were starving. It was the best morning of camp *ever*.

As we dashed for the showers, a red car pulled up. Mr. Murphy and another man got out. Then it hit us like a cannonball.

It was CROMWELL!

NO!!!!! NO!!!!! NO!!!!! NO!!!!! *HOW COULD THEY DO THIS TO US?*

I got a pain in the stomach. Honestly! Cromwell at camp was like Darth Vader at your birthday party. How could they send him to us at this perfect place? It was cruel!

The news flashed around the camp: "The *BOMB* is here!"

"What a BUMMER! NO!!!!! NO!!!!! NO!!!!! TOTAL UNBONUS!!!!!"

But it was true.

The fun evaporated.

Jonah went quiet.

21 | GLUMBINYA

"Hello, Brian," said Miss Cappelli in a bright voice, as if she was making friends for the first time. "Welcome to the past!" She waved her arm at all the old buildings and sheds. If she was acting, it was a good act. You can feel it with some of the teachers. They put on an act with him. Chook, Lisa, and Miss Cappelli seemed to be offering friendship, as if they were starting all over again.

The Bomb carried his bags to the teachers' hut.

"This'll be interesting," said Mitch.

But The Bomb didn't sleep there. He slept in a little hut about a hundred meters from them. All by himself.

Mary heard the car and came out to meet him. "Welcome to Gumbinya." Little Petal growled quietly. Mary picked her up.

The Bomb leaned toward them. "What a lovely little dog!" he breathed.

Little Petal went crazy, snapping, snarling, and twisting in Mary's arms. She wriggled free and raced away down the track with her ears flat and her tail between her legs.

"Little Petal's had an alcoholic master," announced Jonah, then he walked off up the hill with his hands in his pockets, kicking a stone.

"Anyone for fireworks?" said Mitch. We knew there'd be trouble.

"Why would Mrs. Furgus send The Bomb to camp?" Wormz took an angry bite of his second apple.

"Maybe to freshen him up a bit?" said Azza.

"There's two people at this camp that don't fit in," said Mitch.

"Shut up. Great friend you are!" said Nicko.

"Well, he behaves like a saint," said Mitch. "The Bomb gives him heaps, and he just takes it."

"Do you think he *likes* copping it?" said Azza.

"Everyone, *shut up!*" I said.

"I bet The Bomb is here so he can get Jonah," said Azza.

Wormz spat out an apple pip. "We've got to keep Jonah off the target range."

"Mission Impossible!" goes Mitch. "He's in the open." Sometimes Mitch says mean things, but he *does* good things.

"I think we should have a signal," said Azza, throwing his apple core an incredible distance, just missing a donkey's ear.

"What, like a whistle?" said Nicko.

"I know!" said Wormz. "An owl hoot! *Tooowit towoooo! Tooowit towoooo!*"

We all groaned.

"How about this?" goes Nicko, and he starts singing "Advance Australia Fair," except instead of words he sings, "Boom boom boom boom boom boom, boom boom."

"Good one!" said Mitch.

"Okay, that's the signal," said Nicko. "Sing anything you like, in booms."

MEATLOAF

There is one thing that is absolutely top priority at camp, even if The Bomb is exploding and the world is ending—FOOD!

We went to a horse riding camp once and the food was so revolting nobody would eat it. The slops bin was overflowing with gray objects called vegetables.

This being a pioneer camp, the food was different. The cooking was done on two fires. Helmut carted the wood. "Bit different from cooking on a stove," said Edwina, heaving on another log. "You can't twiddle a knob."

Edwina was the cook. She was little, with muscly legs. She came from Manchester, and she had four sisters. Nobody else in her family had ever been out of England. She loved rock climbing and wore tight fluorescent clothes. I could just imagine her like a tiny pink spider on a cliff, climbing her way to the top. She did a great imitation of the Beatles talking, and the stud in her nose was a guitar. With Edwina, everybody was "mate." She loved saying it, and making billy tea in an old powdered milk can over the fire.

Edwina hopped round the fires like a bright little witch, stirring in this pot, sprinkling into that pot, adding and tasting. The cooking groups made this fantastic campfire bread called damper, one with raisins, and another one with cheese.

Every day, Edwina put out a huge basket of crisp apples and a plastic tank of fruit punch that wasn't too watery. We could help ourselves anytime. Sometimes we were really hungry.

"Look for the cook!" goes Wormz.

"Edwina, we're *starving!*"

Then she would give us a big hunk of damper slathered with butter, or a carrot to gnaw on.

We knew why the donkeys were always hanging over the fence in our direction!

At supper the hot chocolate had real milk and lots of chocolate, not like the horse camp, where it was 99% water, ½% milk, and ½% chocolate.

Everybody loved the fires. The main campfire had a ring of rocks around it, and behind that a ring of old chairs. You could sit on the chairs with your feet on the rocks. I love watching things burn, and burning things, but I'm never allowed to do it at home.

Cooking-duty group had to report to the cookhouse more than an hour before the meal. There was a lot to do. Actually, it was the Explorers' turn, but Miss Cappelli swapped us. "She wants us out of the way," said Nicko.

Edwina gave us plastic buckets and ice cream containers. "Fill that with peas, that full of tomatoes, this one full of beans, and four lettuces. Okay, mates, let's go!"

Down beyond the old buildings, there was the lush green veggie patch, standing out vividly against the dull gray bush. Beans, sweet corn, tomatoes, lettuce, onions, carrots, lots of green herbs—everything was growing like mad.

"Hey, Nicko, tried the peas?" yelled Azza.

"Yeah. They're delicious!"

"I just ate one without picking it. In the pod. Just bit it off."

"This is the Garden of Eden," said Mitch.

"Try the beans!" said Wormz. "You can eat them straight off the plant, too." Wormz was grazing like an animal.

79

"Hey, mates, leave some!" laughed Edwina. "Everybody else is hungry, too, you know."

"Who looks after the veggie garden, Edwina?" asked Nicko.

"Everyone: students, travelers, Brownies, Cub Scouts, Mary, people who come and stay for a while."

"Hey, check it *out!*" yelled Wormz suddenly. "This is a *major* pumpkin!"

Growing by the back fence was the most enormous pumpkin we had ever seen—Cinderella's coach, life-size! The pumpkin's dying leaves covered the fence and trailed over it, back down the hill.

"How did it ever grow so big?" asked Azza.

"It's near the drain," said Edwina. "Good soil, sun."

Mary and Naomi came through the garden gate.

"Mary, did you know about the humongous pumpkin?"

"Yes. The last school called him Meatloaf. Is he ripe yet?"

"How do you know when he's ripe?" asked Nicko.

"What do you think?" said Mitch. "He says, 'I'm ready!'"

"He says, 'Excuse me, you can eat me now!'" said Azza.

Edwina looked at us. She looked at the pumpkin's dried-up stem. She looked at Mary, who grinned and nodded. She made a decision. "Okay, mates, today's the day for that big boy."

"Today is the day of his destiny," spouted Naomi. Once she starts, you can't stop her. "The fine, proud, golden king burns with color in the sea of his withering leaves. The tendrils which fed him wither and die while he sits proud and awaits his fate."

"We need a forklift, a crane, a pick-up truck, and a chain saw," said Jonah.

"I've got a wheelbarrow," said Mary.

We tried to lift him, but he wouldn't budge! There was nothing to grab on to.

"Pick him up by the stem," suggested Wormz.

"*You* pick him up by the stem," said Mitch.

We got Helmut.

Then, with everyone helping, in one mighty heave, we got Meatloaf into the wheelbarrow.

"Come on, Meatloaf. We're taking you for a lovely little ride."

"Make way for the King of Vegetables."

"Make way for Meatloaf the Big Boy."

Helmut walked on one side and two kids on the other, making sure Meatloaf wouldn't tip over. We trundled all the way to the cookhouse, then we had to wait while kids got their cameras and took photos of him.

"Smile, Meatloaf!"

"Only one problem with this," said Miss Cappelli. "They hate pumpkin."

"Big pumpkins don't have so much flavor," said Mary. "The smaller ones with the golden color have the real sweet pumpkin flavor."

"Could be good that it doesn't have the pumpkin flavor," said Miss Cappelli.

"How will we cut him up?" asked Nicko.

"With an ax."

"Chain saw."

"See that stone step by the table?" said Mary. "I suggest we drop him on that."

We scrubbed the step, then we heaved Meatloaf up onto the table and pushed him off. He gave a shuddering bounce.

"I can see a crack!" yelled Wormz. "See! On the step!"

We groaned.

"Again."

We heaved Meatloaf up, washed the stone because we'd stood on it, and dropped him again, just missing Nicko's foot.

"Careful, Nicko!" said Edwina. "I'd hate to have to ring up your mum and say, 'Sorry, mate, he got squashed by a pumpkin.'"

Three times we pushed Meatloaf off the table, and the third time, he split.

"They fell upon his noble broken body and slashed with swords and zeal," spouted Naomi, "till naught was left but pyramids of pumpkin skin and a cauldron of chunky gold."

"And Nicko's finger with a Band-Aid!" added Nicko.

The pumpkin simmered in the pot. We stirred and stirred. The big golden chunks got soft. Edwina sat by the fire, chopping up onions and clove after clove of garlic and throwing them in. It cooked until at last it was blobbing gold mud. Like porridge boiling, the bubbles slowly plopped.

We were all sitting round the fire by this time, and Lisa was reading us a book called *War Horse,* which was terribly sad, and some kids were sniffing. But kids watching the pot were laughing. She stopped before the end of the chapter, closing the book. "I can't compete with Meatloaf."

"It's golden sun lava," said Naomi.

"It's a magic brew for naughty children who won't eat their vegetables," said Melanie.

"Volcanoes vomited vitamins," spouted Nicko.

Then The Bomb walked into the firelight and killed the poetry stone dead. Mary, who was over by the ship's bell, looked up to see

Smile Meatloaf!!

why the laughing stopped. She watched The Bomb.

?????

Actually, a lot of that pumpkin got eaten. Some of it went into the slops. But one thing you know with Mary, eventually everything gets eaten, by the chickens, or Little Petal, or the horse, or the donkeys, or Mintie.

"I prefer eggs to pumpkin," said Azza. "I'm leaving my soup for the chickens."

Wormz had three helpings.

I've still got one of Meatloaf's seeds in my shorts pocket.

23 AZZA'S LEG

Sometime in the night, I woke up. One of us was crying.

"Had a nightmare, Azza?" came a whisper.

"My leg hurts," he sniffed in a very un-Azza voice.

"You might have been bitten by a snake and you never knew it!" said Wormz.

"Shut up, will you," goes Azza. "It's not funny. It's damn hurting. It's damn, damn hurting!" (Only he wasn't saying damn.)

"Maybe it's a heart attack," said Wormz.

"You can't have a heart attack in your leg, derr brain," said Nicko.

"What about a stroke in your leg? My grandfather died of a stroke," said Wormz.

"Cancer of the leg?"

"Just shut up, will you. He's in agony," said Mitch.

Azza isn't a wimp.

"Let's have a look at your leg," said Jonah.

Azza undid his sleeping bag and held up the hurting leg. We all inspected it, but it looked fine.

"Can you move it?" asked Wormz.

"Well, he's holding it up, isn't he?" said Mitch.

"Can you move your toes?" said Nicko.

"Yeah. It's been damn hurting for damn, damn ages."

"What? Like all week?" said Wormz.

"No, for hours."

A light flashed in, blinding us, followed by a *whoosh* of alcohol vapor like a dragon's breath. Oh, great! Oh, wonderful! Oh, blessings! The Good Doctor Cromwell. Now everything will be all right!

"What's going on here?" His flashlight flickered around because he couldn't keep it steady, flashing full in our faces. When the blinding light fell on Jonah's face, he grunted.

"Mr. Cromwell, Azza's got a really bad pain in his leg," goes Mitch.

"Give me a look," says The Bomb.

"There's nothing you can see," sniffs miserable Azza.

"Which leg is it, then?" The Bomb flashes the light around as he wobbles to stay standing up.

"Not that one," says Nicko.

"Well, which leg is it, then?" snaps The Bomb, getting nasty.

When there are two legs, and you're looking at the *wrong* one, you don't have to be a genius to figure out which is the right one. That describes the fat lot of good The Bomb was. Besides, if you'd lit a match when he breathed out, the tent would have exploded. I hated him and his stinking alcoholic stupidity.

"Did something bite you?"

"I don't think so."

"There's nothing wrong with that leg. Don't be such a wimp. You must have pulled a muscle or something. Cramp. Go to sleep. Stop disturbing everybody. And the rest of you—" He looked around for Jonah, but Jonah wasn't there, or maybe he couldn't see him, or he forgot what he was doing. (I was trying to guess how he was going to blame Azza's leg on Jonah.) "If I hear one more sound from this tent, you're in it, *deep!*"

The blinding flashlight went out and we heard him stumping away.

Azza sniffed quietly. "Well, at least he didn't rip Jonah to bits."

"Where is Jonah?" goes Wormz.

"Must have gone for a leak," said Nicko.

A couple of minutes later, another flashlight bobbed into the tent. This time, a little plastic yellow one. It was Jonah with Chook.

Chook was in her bathrobe. Her face looked puffy and wrinkled. She'd just woken up and looked much older. Her smell was nice, like a mum...powder or perfume or something.

Sitting on the edge of Azza's bunk, she could see how miserable he was. "Dear me, you poor old fellow." Chook had a good look at the leg. We were all taking in the events. "The rest of you get back to your dreams." Gently, she rubbed Azza's leg. "Does this hurt?"

"No."

"Has it ever hurt like this before?"

"No."

"Well, you know what I think?" said Chook quietly. "It's growing pains. I don't know what causes them, but they're nothing to worry about. My Paul got them at about your age. He's twenty-two now and plays rugby for Dandenong. You're just growing bigger, that's all."

Suddenly, there's a roar and a blinding flash of light. *"LISTEN, YOU LITTLE VERMIN, WHAT DID I SAY? GET THAT FLASHLIGHT OFF! AND WHAT ARE YOU DOING HERE, YOUNG LADY? GET BACK TO YOUR TENT!"* The light is on Chook. He thinks she's one of the *girls!*

Chook, eyes wide, gasps, "Brian!"

The Bomb steadies himself on the tent pole and flicks his flashlight right into her face. "Oh...it's you, Betty."

"Get that light off me. Mario's got a sore leg."

"There's nothing wrong with it."

Chook bristles like an angry rooster. "Brian, you leave this to me. Why don't you go and…"(we silently add, Drop dead, Fall off a cliff, Drown, Hang yourself, Blow up)"…sleep."

The Bomb stumbled out, growling under his breath, tripping over Mitch's stick.

"By jingo," muttered Chook, "he's the one that needs the treatment!"

"My leg's not so bad now," said Azza.

"Good man," said Chook. "I could give you an aspirin, but I'm sure you'll be fine in the morning. If it's too sore, Jonah, you come and get me again. Now, all of you. Off to sleep."

She left in a waft of the mum smell. It was dark and quiet again.

"That old Chook…she's not so bad," whispered Nicko. Mitch was already asleep.

The next morning was a whole new day, and Azza was fine.

Somebody overheard somebody who told Mitch that The Bomb said Jonah squealed on him to Chook.

24 NICKO'S DREAM

Nicko's mattress was tipped right off the bunk, and Nicko, who sleeps like a log, was gone.

"He's Nicko-ed off!" said Mitch.

"I found him!" yelled Azza from down the hill. "He's under a bush! Still asleep!"

Nicko's sheet, sleeping bag, pajamas, arms, legs, and everything were twisted in a sweaty knot, like stuff from the washing machine after a mega spin dry.

"What happened, Nicko, my man?" said Mitch.

"Oh gosh…oh gee…oh…ah…ahhh…oh…" (Nicko takes a while to wake up.) "Oh gosh…I had this dream…I was in that arcade, Time Zone. There was a free play on Primal Rage. It said, 'Play if you dare!' Someone hadn't taken it.

"It was awesome. I was playing like a professional. To get energy, you had to eat all these smaller dinosaurs, then a massive dinosaur comes on roaring, with teeth as long as my arm and two rows of huge spikes on its back. It clawed its victim, then it rolled on it with its spikes. You could hear the bones cracking.

"Then I smelled something strange. Blood! I looked down and my arm was missing and I was squirting blood from my shoulder. Suddenly, the big dinosaur lunged at me with The Bomb's glare in its eyes. I was fighting for my life. Both my arms were in the machine, and my hands were claws. Lights were flashing, like in *Gladiators*.

"I was still playing really well. And I got the highest score in the world on that game. And I put my initials on it. Then I woke up."

"Wow!" goes Azza. "You shouldn't read any more horror books, you should *write* them!"

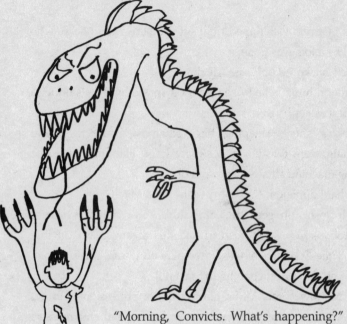

"Morning, Convicts. What's happening?" It was Miss Cappelli, Lisa, and Mr. Murphy.

"Nicko sleeprolled!" said Mitch.

He looked such a fright, with sticks and grass in his hair, the adults cackled.

"Oh, Nicko, don't get yourself in such a knot!" said Lisa.

"When you've untied yourself, have a shower," said Miss Cappelli. "You'll be late for breakfast, but we'll save you a baked bean."

25 BLOODY LEECHES

This morning's activity was leech torture, although it was called a half-day hike to see a gold mine.

I'll tell you something about hiking, trekking, and bush-whacking—they're fancy names for walking. Up front were Miss Cappelli, Lisa, and Chook with a crowd of kids buzzing around them, and at the back, totally solo, was The Bomb.

"Walk in a blob please, not a snake," said Chook.

Some kids saw leeches waving themselves near the path, in a frenzy.

"You'd wave, too, if you were a leech," said Mitch. "How would you like hanging around in the bush waiting for breakfast for yonks and yonks? I bet there are thousands of leeches who never even get their first suck of blood before they die. There's a lot of bush and a lot of leeches, and not many creatures."

"Millions of leeches, leeches for me," sang Azza, juggling a stick.

"Wonder if leeches suck other leeches in desperation?" said Nicko. "Say there's this lucky leech and he gets a good half an hour on the leg of this muscly sports teacher. Man, he is one fat roly-poly leech. He's feeling fabulous. How are all the skinny little leech dudes going to feel? Do they do leech peer support? Is the fat leech going to say to the little skinnies, 'Hey, guys, do you want some? Dig in.'"

It started sprinkling rain, slowly getting us soaking wet. Perfect leech weather. We plodded on. If The Bomb caught up, Jonah

Hey Dudes!! I found a gold nugget!!!
That's a chicken nugget!!
Leeches!!!
Is that you?
No! It's me!
I need to go to the toilet!
OW! get off my foot!

dropped back, if The Bomb dropped back, Jonah caught up. If The Bomb was on the left of a bunch of kids, Jonah was on the right. Maybe nobody else noticed, but Miss Cappelli did. She gave us a wink.

We reached the gold mine, which was a hole in the hill with blackberries growing over the front. The rain was getting a bit heavier now.

Fifty-one juicy, saturated city kids come to a halt. We are sitting ducks! Leech bait! Every leech for 50 kilometers hears the leech cry, *"KIDS AT THE MINE! FRESH KIDS! FRESH KIDS!"* A wave of leeches starts looping full pelt toward us.

Only fifteen kids at a time can go into the mine. You have to crouch down, holding on to the sweater of the person in front, and shuffle along with your knees bent. It's pitch-black, and you keep bumping into people. Someone said there were black widow spiders hanging off the roof. And glowworms. I saw them, but their batteries were flat.

Then we got to a dead end, and everyone sat on top of each other in the dark. Chook shone a flashlight and told us it was the end of the mine. This was pretty obvious because we were looking at a wall of rock. It was a bit sad, really, because we were looking at where the miner ran out of hope and said, "I give up."

Meanwhile, outside in the rain, the leech feast had begun! Leeches on cheeks, down necks, on boots, on socks, on lips, on legs, waving and looping. Some of them are skinny, like fine threads, some of them are swelling blobs.

"Hey, guys, look at this!" yells Nicko. A leech is sucking from an artery on the back of his hand. He pumps his hand and he's *pumping up the leech!* Awesome! You can *see* the leech *swelling!*

Then, out of the dripping bush stumbles The Bomb. He sees Nicko. "Stop that, you stupid idiot." He whacks the pumped-up leech off Nicko's hand and it splatters a bloody mess over his own pale brown parka.

The Bomb would like to splatter Nicko the way he splattered the leech. Fortunately, Chook's mob comes out of the mine in the nick of time. The Bomb slips and slides down to the creek to wash off Nicko's blood.

Mrs. Pumps-Vital, who's looking pretty anxious herself, keeps saying, "It's all right! It's all right!" in a voice that sounds like, "It's not all right! It's not all right!"

Kids are crying. They want to be home sitting on Mummy's knee in front of the telly with a hot cocoa, but they're here with leeches waving off them.

Girls are screaming like car alarms, kids are jumping round trying to look on their backs, shaking their hands, doing this Michael Jackson leech dance. They are flicking, scraping, pulling, brushing, screaming: *"GET IT OFF! GET IT OFF!"* You flick it with one hand—it sticks to the other hand. You *can't* get them off. You know what? Leeches stick like leeches!

Jonah is calm. He has about five kids around him and he's picking off their leeches, not worrying about his own. "Leeches are really interesting," he says. "Australia used to export leeches from the Murray River. They were sold in drugstores. If you put a leech on a bruise, it takes down the swelling."

"Dudes, we are being seriously annihilated here," says Azza.

"Yeah," says Wormz, "we're going to need three helpings of dessert to make up for lost blood."

I got a leech on my ear.

"Hey, dude, what's that groovy earring you've got on your ear?" said Mitch.

"My leech."

"Cool ring," said Azza, putting one on his nose.

"Yeah," said Wormz, "we're Leech Boys."

Wonder if you can train leeches?

Chook produces two packets of mints, and we squelch off back to camp. Four kilometers of soggy, slippery, bush track sustaining heavy continuous leech bombardment. There's stacks of nature, like tree ferns and fungi, but we're too busy fighting off the attack of the brown slinkies.

Back at camp, we Number Off to see how many kids have survived the ordeal.

"I'm zero," goes Miss Cappelli.

"I'm dead!" goes Mitch.

Everyone survived.

The Bomb is throwing stones at a stump. He misses four times. Pretty pathetic for an archery ace. Mrs. Pumps-Vital looks like a drowned duck. Lisa's wet hair makes her look like one of the Addams Family. Mr. Murphy is getting the total plot of *Star Trek: The Next Generation* from Tak. Mitch goes, "I'm so hungry I could eat a leech!"

We jumped under the showers. I was still washing the mud out of my ears when I found a cute little baby leech under my arm. So I called him Terminator and stuck him in my empty shampoo bottle and took him home as a pet.

I wonder how you breed them? For my next free-choice project I'm going to do: "The Life of a Leech."

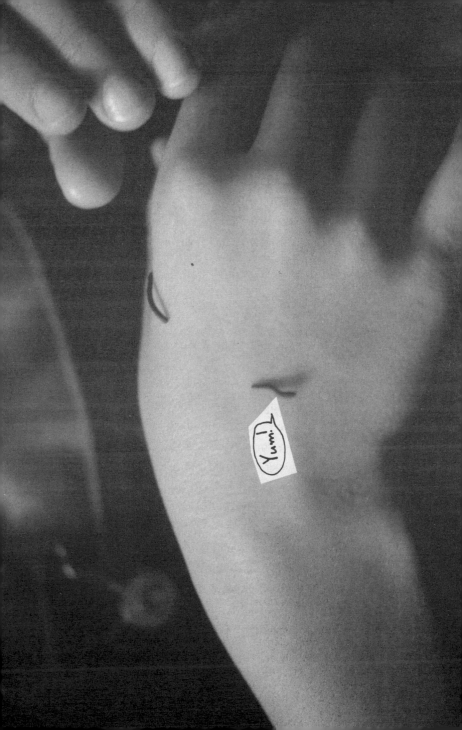

26 THE FEATHER

On the hike, Jonah found a feather. It was long and strong, like the ones they wrote with in medieval days. He said it was from an eagle. One of the wing-tip steering feathers that you see spread out like fingers in the wind.

Jonah got his pocketknife (which you weren't supposed to have at school camp), cut two small holes in his black hat, and stuck the feather through.

It looked so cool.

Up comes The Bomb. "Get that stupid feather off your head."

Jonah didn't move.

"We're not in school uniform now, Mr. Cromwell," goes Azza. "We're at camp."

"I said, *get that stupid feather off your head.*"

Still, Jonah did nothing. Didn't even look at The Bomb.

Nicko pipes up, "It's cool, Mr. Cromwell. We can wear anything at camp as long as we're sunsmart. Actually, it's an eagle's feather from the end of the wing," thinking he could change the subject with facts.

The Bomb glared at Jonah. Jonah didn't look at him. I thought The Bomb was going to grab the feather and chuck it, but he turned and walked off.

Ten minutes later, as we were filing into the dining hut for lunch, The Bomb stood just inside the door. Jonah saw him a split second too late. The Bomb grabbed the feather, cracked it, and chucked it in the bin. "Get your hat off!" he snapped at Jonah.

Other kids came in and didn't take their hats off until they were sitting at the table, and The Bomb didn't say anything to them.

"Rotten slime bucket orang-outang!" goes Mitch under his breath.

But after lunch, Jonah appeared wearing the broken feather in his hat. He'd fished it out of the trash, washed it, and stuck it back in his hat. And there it stayed.

Miss Cappelli called him Brave Broken-Feather, and the nickname stuck.

ꟻꟻꟻꟻꟻ

"Listen to this!" goes Nicko in a shout-whisper, waving madly at me. We were going round the back of the teachers' hut to our tent to get our Camp Journals.

"Goodness gracious!" said Chook.

"This is school camp!" We could hear Miss Cappelli's voice getting louder and angrier. "It's supposed to be *fun!* It's the one time of the year when we all go away together. We learn things and we *enjoy* ourselves. Stop *picking* on him."

Mr. Murphy muttered something.

Mrs. Pumps-Vital, for the first time in her life, was quiet.

The Bomb's voice, deeper than usual, muttered something.

"You're wrong!" I heard Lisa say.

"...needs to smarten his act up...the boy's a gutless little wimp."

"No, Brian, he's strong," said Miss Cappelli, "like you!"

Then we shot off because someone opened a door.

ꟻꟻꟻꟻꟻ

A bit later, The Bomb made Jonah sit by himself on the steps of the cookhouse for some reason. Mary happened along and sat down, too, for a chat—about animals, I bet. The Bomb couldn't tell her off for talking to him!

27 STICK-AND-SPUD SPINNING

In the afternoon we had to pick between spinning, blacksmithing, making damper, and making butter. We chose blacksmithing.

Suddenly, Miss Cappelli appeared and said in a don't-ask-me-why voice, "You Convicts are spinning."

"Guess what activity The Bomb's in charge of!" said Nicko.

"Thanks, Jonah," said Mitch.

It had stopped raining, but everything was damp. Mary sat on the veranda of the rec hall. "The first settlers had to carry their belongings a long way," she said. "They decided very carefully what to bring with them. They could still spin, without a spinning wheel, as long as they had a stick and a potato. Get me that stick by the tree please, Matos."

Mary picked a spud from the bucket beside her, stuck the stick through it, and showed us how to spin. You grab a lump of Mintie's wool and fluff it out and comb it with the bed-of-nails bats. We worked in pairs. One person is the teaser-outer and the other is the spud-spinner.

Then, when it's fluff fluff fluffy, you twist it onto the thread from the spud, and you spin the spud and feed the fluff out.

stick

spud

Jonah and I couldn't get the knack at first. Our thread kept breaking, then it was too lumpy. "Tease it more," said Mary.

We got the knack.

We thought spinning would be boring, but it was cool fun. Mary told us about her sister who was in a race to shear a sheep, spin the wool, and knit it into a sweater. It took nine hours!

Jonah said the fishermen of Aran wear the same sweaters all their lives, and if they drown and a body is washed up, people can tell who it is by the pattern of their sweater. "They're bad news for the fashion industry!" laughed Mary. Jonah smiled at her.

First Jonah spun the spud, then we swapped. "Let's make it really fine," said Jonah. "Twist slow and steady."

He fed out the wool. We got it thin and even, like a real length of yarn.

Then the ship's bell rang, and it was time for duty groups. Jonah pulled off our finest piece of thread and stuck it in his overalls pocket. I'd been thinking I would take it home to show Mum. I didn't say anything, but I was annoyed.

26 MORE TROUBLE THAN THE EARLY SETTLERS

There were shouts from the Swaggies' tent: "Thornton Primary's done a wee on Christianna's pillow!"

"And Little Petal's eaten my...Oh, nothing!"

Naomi lugged Thornton Primary out and put him down on his four stumpy legs. "Guilty!" she said.

He scratched a wombat flea and headed back to the Swaggies' tent.

"No you don't!" said Naomi.

There was a big blow-up about the Swaggies still having candy. Renee's bag was ripped.

Then there was the medicine bottle smash.

Before camp, your parents filled in a form about asthma, wetting the bed, etc. If you had to take medicine, it was kept in the teachers' fridge and they supervised it.

"I have to take my medicine now," said Sarah to Miss Cappelli, who was helping with cooking-duty group.

"Good, Sarah, go and get it. I trust you."

She was standing outside the teachers' hut when The Bomb yelled behind her, "What do you think you're doing?" She dropped the bottle and it smashed on the concrete step. There was a big fuss.

"It doesn't matter. I'm nearly better," said Sarah. "Honestly, I could do without the last of it."

"No," goes The Bomb. "You have to take the lot. I caused her to drop it. I'll go and get the replacement."

So he drove off to the next town, which is a fair way.

"He'll get some medicine from Auntie Boozer as well!" said Mitch.

Then everyone tucked into the apples. Matos, the show-off, took his apple core to Sinbad, the horse, and like a dumb idiot he horsed around with the horse. Sinbad bit Matos on the nose!

Matos was groaning in agony. Mary, Lisa, and Miss Cappelli ran to him.

"The one time we really need that man, he isn't here," said Chook. The Bomb had just driven off in the in-case-of-emergencies car.

"I'm not waiting till he gets back," said Miss Cappelli. "He could take ages. This boy's in agony. He's got to see a doctor."

"Okay," said Mary. "Helmut's got my car. We'll have to take him in my bus. I think Doctor Connor is our best bet. That's about thirty k's."

As well as horse-drawn carts and wagons, Mary had an old school bus.

Chook made some phone calls, then Mary hopped up behind the big steering wheel and started up her old bus. Miss Cappelli sat beside poor Matos, who was holding an ice pack on his nose and clutching a box of tissues.

"Good luck!" we yelled as the massive old bus with two little passengers bumped off down the drive and swung onto the highway.

"I know it was a terrible misfortune," said Wormz. "I know it hurts Matos like mad, but gee, that was funny!"

29 KITCHEN DUTY

Dinner was barbecued chicken and salad (not all gooed up with dressing), followed by chocolate mousse, which we called moose.

"How was it?" asked Edwina. She always wanted to know what we thought.

"Wicked!" we said.

According to our camp books, the Convicts were on kitchen duty with Miss Cappelli supervising, so we thought we might get a special guest appearance by The Bomb. He still hadn't shown up with Sarah's medicine.

We knew what we had to do—scrape the plates into the slops bucket, wash everything, stack it, and put it away. No worries. Easy peasy. We swung into the job. There wasn't much going into the slops bucket. Everybody had eaten their moose. *Clatter, clatter, crash, bang.* All the plates were scraped and stacked.

Nicko turned on the hot tap over the huge silver sink. Azza squeezed detergent into it. It frothed up a bit.

"That's not enough," said Nicko. He grabbed the big plastic detergent bottle and gave it a mighty squeeze. The top came off, and a mass of detergent whooshed out.

"Yoweee!!!!!!" goes Nicko. "That should be enough!"

"Too much!" says Azza.

"No, it's a big sink. It needs lots," said Nicko.

"Not *that* much," said Azza.

"Everything is hunky and dory," said Nicko.

Then the suds frothed up, foaming like a cloud, swelling out of the sink.

"Hey, that reminds me of the Sorcerer's Apprentice in *Fantasia*, where Mickey can't stop the water coming out of the well," said Mitch.

"Cool!" said Wormz.

Then the foam flowed over the edge of the sink.

"Not so cool!" said Wormz.

The water was really hot now, gushing down hard into the ever-rising foam.

"Turn it off, Nicko! *Turn it off!*" yelled Azza.

He turned it off. "Now what?"

"Wash the dishes," said Mitch.

"What? In that pile of bubbles?"

"Not in the bubbles, in the water, dope."

"I think we should get rid of this water and get some new, not-so-hot water," said Wormz.

"Yeah, good idea," said Jonah.

Nicko put his hand into the bubbles and pulled it out again with a screech. "Ahhhhhhhhh!!!!! It's boiling! I'm not putting my hand in there!"

"Now what do we do?" said Azza.

"Put in cold water to cool it down." Jonah was practical.

"Brilliant!" Azza put his hand into the bubbles, found the cold tap, and turned it on. But two seconds later, bubbles and water started flowing over the edge of the sink.

"We'll have to wait till it cools down," said Azza.

"No, scoop up the bubbles in a bucket and take them out the door to the drain," said Jonah.

Mitch stood on a stool and fished around in the cloud of froth with a long pair of barbecue tongs, trying to get the plug out. At last he did. The water drained away. It took ages to wash away the bubbles.

We started again with hot, not boiling, water, and just the right amount of detergent. Everything went smoothly, except when Wormz put a whole pile of plates into the sink.

"They're clean ones, *dope!*" snapped Azza.

"They were *with* the dirty ones, *dope!*" snapped Wormz.

We were doing a good job. We had the glasses done, the cutlery, and most of the plates. The tea towels were absolutely saturated. Jonah was putting the stacks away.

Suddenly, *"Boom boom. Boomba boom boom,"* goes Nicko loudly, to the tune of *The Flintstones*.

A dramatic guest appearance! The Bomb charged in. "Hurry up! You were supposed to be finished half an hour ago. Just as well I checked on you."

He strode to where Jonah was stacking glasses. There was an almighty crash. Three stacks of six glasses smashed on the concrete floor.

"You stupid, clumsy…Clean up the mess! You'll pay for this, and you're on permanent kitchen duty till you learn to be a bit more careful."

Jonah got the trash can. I got the dustpan and the brush. Jonah was like a robot. "He knocked me."

"Don't worry, Jonah," I whispered.

"And this bench is filthy. Clean it!" yelled The Bomb. "And when it's clean, clean it again!"

30 LETTER HOME

Dear Mum......Was there someone else? Oh yes.
My ugly brother Adrian.

Greetings!!!!!!!!!!

Camp is cool. Except for one thing.
Ill tell you when I get home.
We are the Convicts, and we have the best tent.
The food is great. Not slops. Mum, don't worry.
I am being very careful with my camera.
I carry it in my back pack. Just wait till you
see the snaps!!!!!

There are two ~~two~~ wombats here called Bulldozer
and ~~Adrian~~ Thornton Primary, but we are not
allowed to pat them.
A horse bit Matos's nose. All the daub got
washed out of our wattle.

Give my love to the T.V. Tell it I will ~~be~~ home
on Friday.

Love from Mark (Mark)

P.S. If my Venus Fly Trap has indigestion
Adrian, you're in for it!

108

34 TALK IN DARKNESS

Before the night hike, Mr. Murphy told us about night vision—how you can see at night because your pupils, the black centers of your eyes, open wider to let in more light at night. Like my camera.

We set off without our flashlights because they would wreck our night vision. At first we couldn't see a thing, then our pupils did their job.

There was a dark shape in front of the dam.

"Look, a rat swimming in the water," said Mitch.

"That's not a rat, it's a duck," said Nicko.

"It's not a duck, it's a rat."

"Quack!" said the black shape.

"See, it's a duck!"

"No, it's a rat that speaks duck!"

Chook told them to shut up.

Eventually, we got over the excitement of stumbling around in the dark and saw some possums, an owl, and a lot of stars. There were bursts of bright moonlight, blotted out by sudden thick clouds. One second you could see very clearly, then suddenly, it was pitch-black.

?!?!!!

Later, in the tent, our pupils didn't want to shut down.

"I can't get to sleep," said Wormz.

"Try harder. Threaten yourself," said Mitch. "Tell yourself, 'If I don't go to sleep, I will punch myself in the head.'"

"Mary and Miss Cappelli and Matos have been gone for ages," said Nicko.

"And The Bomb went out again, too," said Jonah.

"What?" We couldn't believe it.

"I'm positive," said Jonah.

"That means there's only Chook, Lisa, Mrs. Pumps-Vital, and Mr. Murphy to look after us!" said Azza.

"I want my mummy!" said Wormz.

"Have you noticed how Miss Cappelli, Lisa, and Chook and the others aren't including The Bomb in some activities?" said Nicko. "They're trying to keep him out of the way. They give him lists to tick off."

"And they're trying to keep him away from you, Jonah," said Azza.

"Did you see how Miss Cappelli switched us from the blacksmith's?" said Mitch.

"Brian Cromwell is an invertebrate with very limited appeal," said Nicko. "A boil on the bum of mankind!"

"He's past his use-by date," said Azza.

"Pay attention, Whaleman," said Mitch. "We are going to do something about your friend."

"Don't get me into more trouble," said Jonah.

"He's sure to be getting medicine from Auntie Boozer," said Nicko. "He'll be away for ages."

"Wish he'd never come back," said Jonah.

"Let's do something tonight to welcome him home!" said Mitch. We hatched a plan.

"Hey, life! Live it! Slip! Slop! Slap! Just do it!" goes Wormz.

Nicko goes, "My night vision is really strong. I could read a book."

"I could thread a needle," goes Jonah.

"I could braid the hairs in my nose," said Azza.

"Then what are we doing lying here?" said Mitch.

Do you want to hear something funny? Mr. Murphy did the last night prowl, and our tent got the Log Award for settling down well. Not a murmur. I'll tell you why we were so quiet: We weren't there.

Creeping around camp in the dark was so cool—making signals, trying not to wake anybody up. We had to freeze for about five minutes while one of the Squatters went to the toilet. One of the Drovers yelled out, "Wet towels!" in his sleep.

On the path from where The Bomb parked his car to his hut, we constructed a simple welcome-home obstacle course.

"This branch just fell here in the night," whispered Mitch as we dragged it across the track. (Ever tried to drag a dead branch quietly?) Then we heaved some rocks and arranged them artistically along the path.

"Some pebbles to help him find his way home." Mitch was really grooving on it.

But Jonah was unsure. "I don't think we should be doing this."

"After all that creep has done to you," said Nicko.

"Admit it. You are a saint, aren't you?" said Mitch.

"We'll take the blame," said Wormz. "We'll say you were sound asleep."

The amazing thing is, we didn't wake anybody up.

From the highest branches of the huge pine tree at the top of the hill, we could see a long, long way. That was when the moon was out. When it was behind a cloud, we couldn't see a thing.

It was scary and exciting, especially when I was climbing up. I slipped and was just dangling, hanging by my arms near the top.

111

We sat in the waving branches, waiting for the headlights… waiting…and waiting…and waiting…

"This branch is killing me," said Wormz. "My bum's gone numb! I'm going back to bed."

"You can't!" said Mitch.

"Just give it a bit longer," said Nicko.

"He could be hours," said Azza.

"I'll give him one more minute!" said Wormz to Mitch. "Time it on your fancy watch."

"…ten…nine…eight…seven…six…five…four…three…"

We saw headlights turn off the highway and drive slowly toward camp.

"Yess!!!" yelled Nicko.

"It's the bus!" said Azza.

"Not big enough," said Jonah.

"Gentlemen," said Mitch, "we have liftoff!"

The car lights slowed to a crawl, then went up a track, then reversed, then drove on toward camp. We scrambled down the tree. Mostly slithered. Azza stood on Wormz's fingers, I scratched my leg, and Nicko ripped his T-shirt.

We ran quietly round the edge of the tents, then crept up to The Bomb's little hut. The teachers' lodge was pitch-black. Mitch looked at his fancy watch. "It's five past midnight."

The car was parked. Lights out. The hut was dark.

"We missed him," whispered Wormz. "He's made it inside and gone straight to sleep."

"No," whispered Nicko. "He's sitting in the car." As if to prove exactly that, we saw the red glow of a cigarette. We crouched, watching the car.

When the car door opened, it gave us a hell of a fright. The Bomb got out, swaying a bit, and shut the door quietly—well, as quietly as someone who's had a gutful can shut a car door. He made his way in the dark without a flashlight.

He looked stooped and old, stumbling to his lonely little hut.

"He doesn't look too good," whispered Nicko.

"His night vision is *very* poor," said Mitch.

He hit the branch first. Walked straight into it, half crumpling at the knees. He got up again and staggered on, missed part of the path and most of the rocks, except for the last few. I was feeling awful. Earlier it had been funny. Not anymore.

He tripped and fell.

"I'm going to help him," whispered Jonah.

"Don't!" said Mitch. "You're mad!"

I grabbed his arm.

The Bomb heaved himself up. When he reached the steps, he gave a little groan as if he was in pain.

We waited till all was quiet in the hut, and the light was out, then we carted the rocks away and dragged the branch back.

We crept to our tent. No way was The Bomb going to get us tonight.

"How was that groan?"

"You won't believe this," said Mitch, "but I felt sorry for him."

"Yeah," said Nicko.

Jonah said nothing.

Nicko started to speak slowly. "My uncle Michael...was on the booze."

"Yeah?" We were all interested.

"He and Kerry, that was his wife, used to come round for

barbecues. At first he'd be fine, but he'd keep drinking. Kerry'd be saying things like, 'That's enough, Michael!' and 'It's time to go, Michael!' and he'd swear at her. Then Mum said if he couldn't get his act together, she didn't want to know him.

"We didn't see him for ages. Then one Saturday Mum and I went round to his place. It was so gross, *so, so* gross. In the backyard there were bottles everywhere, and he never put his rubbish out. It stank. It was so, so foul. Rotting stuff heaped everywhere. He'd lost his job. Mum and Michael had a great yelling match. And Mum screamed at him that he might as well die.

"Then we went home and got the trailer, came back, cleaned up his mess, and took it to the dump."

"Yeah, then what?" said Wormz.

"Well, he went to this secret club for drunks, can't remember the name."

"Alcoholics Anonymous," said Mitch. "They meet in the scout hall kitchen."

"Yeah, that's it," said Nicko. "Anyway, then he came to tea, about six months later, and he was fine, not swearing or anything. And now he's married to Kay, who's just like Kerry, and they live in Adelaide."

"Why do they do it?"

"Beer tastes so foul they have to get drunk!" said Wormz.

"My uncle Michael was damn miserable," said Nicko.

"You going to get drunk?" said Azza to anybody.

"My brother Wade gets paralytic every Saturday night at parties," said Wormz.

"How do you know? Do you go to the parties?" said Mitch.

114

"He tells me."

"I've seen my dad drunk a few times, but my mum, never," said Jonah.

"I've seen my mum silly," said Wormz.

"That's drunk."

"No it's not. Drunk is when you can't talk properly and you fall down."

"Well, The Bomb is drunk, but he keeps going," said Jonah.

"Mum's friend Rosie gets really funny drunk. She works in a shoe shop and she acts out the customers: 'Do you have a saze threeeeeee in greeeeen, pleeeeeeeeeease?' 'No, madam, but we have a size six in red.'"

"If you drink then drive, you're a bloody idiot," goes Wormz.

"*You're* a bloody idiot and you don't even drink or drive!" goes Mitch. "You're going to be a *double* bloody idiot when you get older!"

"Why do you reckon The Bomb drinks?" goes Nicko.

"To forget how awful he is."

"Because he can't stop."

"So he can be nastier to us kids."

"Who knows? Ask him."

"Mr. Cromwell, can you please tell us why you get drunk?" goes Nicko with big eyes, talking like Faith Williamson.

32 THE TRIP TO THE DOCTOR

Breakfast the next morning was a buzz of stories. The Bomb fronted up. I never thought I'd be pleased to see him, but I had a little fear we might have killed him. He wasn't exactly happy, but he wasn't too bad, considering the night before! The only sign of our obstacle course was a couple of Band-Aids on his hands and some black looks at us.

His story was he had a flat tire and had to change it. You should have seen the look Chook gave him. Mary was the same as ever. Miss Cappelli, tired but laughing, told everyone about the trip to the doctor.

"We drove along the highway, then Mary took a shortcut along a country road. We came to a bridge that the bus couldn't fit under, so we had to reverse a long way to find a place where the bus could turn around.

"I got out and stopped cars while Mary backed the bus on the narrow country road. The ground was soggy from the rain, and the bus slid gently sideways and our back wheels got well and truly bogged.

"The people in the cars, including locals on their way home from rugby practice, got out and helped push the bus. They were joking and laughing about kissing horses. Most of them knew Mary, or they knew about the wombat lady. And sitting in the bus all the time was Matos, in agony, with his bitten nose.

"Eventually, we got to Doctor Connor's. He was out on an emergency, so we had to wait...and wait...and wait...I read to Matos from *New Idea, Who, Woman's Weekly, Thomas the Tank Engine,* and *Where Is Spot?*

"At long last, Doctor Connor arrived and examined Matos's nose and strapped it up. Then Mary drove us home. We stopped to buy a pizza and milkshakes at a late-night cafe.

"Now tell them what's wrong with you, Matos," she said.

Matos grinned under the bandage. "I'b god a brogen doze."

33 CANOEING

I don't like remembering this bit.

In the afternoon, the Convicts, the Settlers, and the Miners had canoeing. This is not pioneering stuff, but Mary organizes horse riding or canoeing if teachers want it.

Without warning, The Bomb strode onto the riverbank and started bossing people around. He told Mandy, the canoeing instructor, that he had a lot of experience. Mandy, who was there just for the day, had never seen any of us before, so she didn't have a clue about The Bomb and Jonah.

There were only two-person canoes. The Bomb put on a life jacket. Nobody wanted to go with him, so we all paired up, quick as lightning. In the muddle and flurry we forgot about protecting Jonah. The Bomb was already in the back of his canoe. Jonah was the only one left.

"Get in, boy," said The Bomb.

I saw the look on Jonah's face, but what could I do? I felt sick.

It was okay until Christian dropped his hat in the water, and it swirled away like a little boat. The river was a slow old thing, but over by the far bank it flowed faster. Jonah and The Bomb were near that part of the river. Jonah reached out his paddle, trying to catch Christian's hat.

"Watch out downstream!" yelled Mandy. "Don't go past the bridge."

"Don't worry!" yelled The Bomb. "I know this river well." They went round the bend. That was the last we saw.

118

I felt sicker.

Mitch yelled to us, "Houston, we have a problem!"

"Don't worry," yelled Azza. "They'll be back any second."

Mandy wasn't worried. She believed The Bomb. She kept teaching us how to canoe.

I watched the bend in the river. "Shouldn't they be back by now?" I yelled to Mandy.

"They'll be fine."

I watched that bend. I watched that bend so hard for the front tip of a canoe, but it didn't come. Finally, Mandy got us out of the river, helmets and life jackets off, and sent us back along the track.

"You come with me," she said to Tommo, and they climbed into a canoe and paddled off down the river.

We raced back to camp to find Miss Cappelli, Lisa, and Chook. We were gasping for breath as we told them what had happened. Miss Cappelli's eyes were wide. Chook clutched her arm.

Then a sodden, ghostlike figure shambled round the corner with his life jacket and his helmet. It was Jonah. There was a great fuss. The teachers were all over him, but he was wet and closed and more non-talking than ever.

"I fell out," he said.

"What about The Bomb?"

"He fell out, too."

"Where is he?"

Jonah shrugged. "I'm going to have a shower."

Miss Cappelli told me to go with him.

"I'm fine!" said Jonah in a cold way. "I can look after myself."

About ten minutes later, a bloke in an old truck turned up with a battered canoe in the back and a half-drowned Cromwell in the front. He looked pretty wobbly. Mr. Murphy and Chook went to help him. Kids crowded around.

"What are you looking at?" croaked The Bomb. "Haven't you seen a wet person before?" He hobbled off to his hut.

We were desperate to know what happened.

"Go and practice your act for the talent show," said Miss Cappelli sharply. "Convicts, you're in the side room of the hall."

‼‼‼

Jonah turned up a bit later, clean and dry but closed as a tough Tubbut nut.

"Come on, Whaleman," said Mitch, "what happened?"

"I fell out."

"Did The Bomb push you?" said Wormz.

"I lost balance and fell out."

"What happened to The Bomb?" said Nicko. "What happened to him?"

"The canoe went over. I dunno. He fell out, too. He got a lift back."

"Why didn't you get a lift back with him?"

"Didn't want to."

"We were scared for you."

"Yeah?"

It was maddening. We knew there was more to the story.

"We'll drop you off the table onto the step to make you open up, like Meatloaf," said Nicko.

"Come on, Jonah, us Convicts are in this together," said Wormz.

"Aren't we your friends?" said Azza.

"Are you?" said Jonah. "Want to share a canoe?"

I felt very low. "Leave him alone," I said.

We gave up. Anyway, we had to get our act together.

34 REHEARSAL

The last night of camp is always a fantastic talent show where we all put on acts.

"*Gladiators!*" goes Mitch.

"Madonna!" goes Wormz.

"*X-Files!*" goes Nicko.

I had seen Helmut behind the toilets with something that gave me an idea. "Pirates!" I said. "Snarling pirate songs, swigging bottles of rum."

"There was Chook, Chook lookin' pretty crook in the store,
> *in the store,*

There was Nicko, sicko, get the bucket quicko, in the quartermaster's
> *store."*

We would be the ugliest, loudest, terrifyingest, funniest hook-handed pirates you have ever seen.

Jonah sat there like a sack of potatoes.

I was determined to have a peg leg.

"Why do pirates have peg legs?" asked Nicko.

"Because they get their legs blown off by cannonballs," said Mitch.

"Why don't they get both legs blown off?"

"No," said Wormz, "sharks bite them off."

"Why do sharks…?"

"Shut up or walk the plank!" said Mitch.

The secret of a good peg leg is one of those giant suction thingies that clears drains and toilets. At home we call it the oompa doompa. You put it on your knee, and it looks really real!

"The search for the hidden treasure of the oompa doompa!" said Nicko.

We found Helmut, old buddy, dearest, best friend Helmut. At first he said he didn't know what we were talking about.

"Oh, come on, Helmut," said Mitch. "Your English is better than ours!"

Then he said he didn't have one.

"Helmut, we saw you with one behind the toilets!"

Then he said he didn't know where it was.

"Helmut, you keep the tools in the locked cupboard in the blacksmith's shed."

Then he said he never let anyone borrow the tools because they never looked after them.

"Helmut, we will look after it so well. We will wrap it in towels and not let anyone touch it. In fact, we will guard it with our lives, and give it back the second the show is over."

Then we said we would fly all his family and uncles and aunts, friends and relations, animals and birds out from Germany for the show and give them the best couches in the rec hall if he would just lend us the oompa doompa.

We followed him around while he dug a drain. After ten minutes, he gave in.

"A pirate went to sea sea sea
with an oompa doompa on his knee knee knee."

Pirate capes were easy: we wore our towels. Nicko had Beauchamp Hotel on his.

We made a parrot by stuffing jocks up Mitch's red socks, then sticking a coat hanger up it and wiring it onto this fabulous crooked branch we found behind the Settlers' tent.

"A pirate went to sea sea sea with a parrot on a tree tree tree."

We took charcoal from the fire, for drawing on beards and mustaches. Nicko got carried away. He put on too much, then wiped his face on Beauchamp Hotel, then decided it was easier to be totally black. He smeared it on, thick, all over. "Ah, me snatches and scratches, I be Black Jack Murzlesmitt."

"A pirate went to sea sea sea, as black as he could be be be."

Still, Jonah wasn't laughing.

Wormz was determined to make Jonah laugh. He went behind the door, then came out with the oompa doompa—stuck on his bum! It was side-splitting! *So, so funny!*

Jonah cracked a grin.

"Atta boy, Jonah, we knew you could do it!" said Azza.

Wormz was so pleased he was dancing around with the oompa doompa wobbling off his bum and tapping a little rhythm on the wall with it.

Then we heard the ship's bell. *Food! Food!!* You could be dying, but if dinner was on the table, forget it!!! Everybody dashed out. Wormz was yelling and screaming, *"I can't get it off!"* The oompa doompa was steadfastly suctioned onto his bum!

Jonah and I went for help.

"It has to be a man!" yelled Wormz.

"Helmut! *Helmut! Come quick.* Wormz's got a problem!"

When we got back, Wormz had bolted the door.

"Who's there?" called the miserable voice of Wormz.

"It's us and Helmut."

He undid the lock and let us in.

Helmut laughed until he went floppy. He nearly split his

purple overalls. "This is the *best* act I have ever seen!" He gave the oompa doompa a hard pull, just like we'd all been doing.

"Oooowww!" yelled Wormz.

"We must break the suction," Helmut said. "Last week we had a kid with his finger caught in a Coke bottle."

After dinner we had an hour to get ready.

Mitch spent ages in front of the mirror, drawing tatts on his arms, with a couple of pens. One said "Death or Golry," but it still looked ace. When he leaves school, he can easily get a job doing tatts. Then he conned Mrs. Pumps-Vital into lending him her gold circle earrings. He looked so cool.

We got tea towels from Edwina for our head scarves. Azza wore his pillowcase because it had sharks on it, and Wormz wore his *Simpsons* underpants with hair sticking out the holes. The scars got a bit out of hand. We used Miss Cappelli's eyebrow pencil. Nicko looked like a victim of rotating knives torture. It's hard to know when to stop.

We got bottles from Helmut, filled them with tea, and stuck RUM on them. Wormz decided he would have fleas and scratch all the time. He also carried a garbage can lid and a board, for some reason. We practiced our songs.

Just before it was time to go, I suctioned the oompa doompa onto my knee with a mixture of spit and water, and tied my leg up to my belt.

"Whaleman, what are you going to do?" said Mitch.

Jonah quietly put on his striped pajama top and the famous black hat with the feather.

35 THE SHOW

Everyone was there: the Queen of England, the President of the United States, Arnold Schwarzenegger…just joking. The teachers and parents sat on the chairs on one side with Mary, Helmut, and Edwina. Miss Cappelli was snazzed up with lipstick and a T-shirt that said JUST HAND OVER THE CHOCOLATE AND NOBODY WILL GET HURT!

The Bomb shambled in, walking like a string puppet. Every step was a jolt. He looked very wonky.

"Are you all right, Brian?" asked Chook.

I had to hop from our tent to the rec hall with my peg leg on. When I arrived, I didn't feel much like a terrible pirate. I felt like someone who wanted to sit down! I crumpled to the floor.

The first act was the Drovers, who did a very boring, squeaky recorder number. And they got it wrong in the middle and had to start again.

Then the Settlers, wearing shower caps and clothes inside out, did a great rock 'n' roll version of "Yes, We Have No Bananas" with words about camp. Everybody joined in at the end, e.g.:

"We have creepies and crawlies
and itchies and scratchies
and ev-ry-thing that bites!
But, yes, we have no bananas,
we have no bananas today."

Then the Miners, who had borrowed everyone's funny big

slippers, did *Playschool,* wearing their pajamas, with their teddies, etc., and talking in that *Playschool* way.

> *"There's a bear in there,*
> *on an electric chair.*
> *There's people with AIDS,*
> *and hand grenades.*
> *Open wide,*
> *commit suicide.*
> *It's Playschool."*

Then they plopped down onto the floor as if they were watching TV and sucked their thumbs.

The Squatters did a really good one. They were a family on holiday on the Gold Coast for the day, at a place like Dreamworld except it was called Wedgie Wonderland. They had their sweat pants pulled up over their shoulders. Things happened, like they'd go on a ride then the Dad would say, "Hey, kids, let's have some fries!"

"No, we can't."

"Why?"

"Because we haven't got any arms." Then they'd all flop on the floor screaming and waving their legs in the air.

Our turn. We must have looked pretty good. Everyone was cheering and yelling and we hadn't even started!

"They're not pirates, they're out of *Mad Max II!*" said Lisa.

"I hope we don't have a mutiny!" said Chook to Mr. Murphy.

"Now, me hearty farties," snarled Nicko, "a few crusty sea

chanteys from me old shipmates to warm you up this cold hard winter's night!"

His parrot fell off.

"Oh no, he's had another bad turn!" goes Nicko.

"He's sensitive to gravity!" yells Wormz, springing on the parrot. "Mouth-to-beak resuscitation!" Honestly, when Wormz goes crazy, you don't know what's going to happen.

"Six pirates went to
    sea sea sea,
As wicked as they
    could be be be."

Azza had a hook. He dropped it and reached out his hand to get it, which got a big laugh. He also had a hunch on his back, and the hunch kept slipping. We just kept on singing and swigging.

"Now, young man," goes Wormz to Helmut, "you have to walk the plank!"

"What did I do?" said Helmut.

"You haven't done anything yet. This is just in case!"

Helmut walked along the board on the floor.

"…and when you get around to doing it, don't *ever* do it again, you hear me?" goes Wormz.

Mitch was swaggering and swashbuckling around.

"Here's a fair young maiden, Miss Minnie Minor," goes Mitch, grabbing Miss Cappelli. "We'll rescue you!"

"But I'm not in any danger!" said Miss Cappelli.

"You are now!" said Wormz. "Walk the plank!"

"But I haven't done anything wrong!"

"Oh, sorry," said Wormz.

"But all that they could see see see were the hairs on the captain's
   knee knee knee.

Helmut came to Oz Oz Oz, the reason is becos 'cos 'cos.

Edwina drank billies of tea tea tea.

She was busting to do a...drawing.

With whiskey cheese and ham ham ham they sailed across the
   dam dam dam."

etc.

Our last song was "The Quartermaster's Store." By this time I was getting really good at walking on my peg leg. Kids said it looked so convincing, like I didn't have a real leg.

Then suddenly, at the end of the song, the wooden part fell out of the rubber part. It made a tremendous clatter as it hit the floor! I hopped sideways, lost my balance and fell on my bum. It was mad. Bits fell off us, but they *loved* it! They thought we *meant* to do it!

We were about to flop back on the couches when Jonah jumped up. Everyone went quiet in a second. There was something about the look of him. He wasn't being a pirate. He wasn't pretending. He started a slow clap, and everyone, still flying with excitement, joined in. He stamped his boot hard, in time with the clap, then, in a strong voice, looking straight at The Bomb, he started to sing:

"What shall we do with a drunken sailor, what shall we do with
   a drunken sailor...?"

Everybody *ROARED!* As loud as fifty-one kids can roar. All the pirates joined in immediately, then everybody, practically lifting the roof off.

Miss Cappelli froze, went white, and stared at her knees. Mrs. Pumps-Vital, eyes wide, poured words into Mr. Murphy's ear. The Bomb stared at Jonah, like a snake trying to mesmerize a mongoose, but Jonah and everybody kept singing at the top of their lungs.

Chook jumped up, waving her hands in the air. "THANK YOU, PIRATES!" she boomed. "Now SETTLE DOWN! Wayne Gardiner, get OFF THAT WINDOWSILL! That is NOT ACCEPTABLE BEHAVIOR! You'd all better SETTLE DOWN! By crikey, you won't be getting any dessert, and Edwina's made you a special cake. Now SETTLE DOWN!"

It took a burst of yelling, but eventually the teachers got us quiet again.

There were a few more items. Paul, Bud, and Pete told some pathetic jokes, and the Settlers did a TV show that started off funny, but they got the giggles and you couldn't really understand it.

Edwina and Lisa did two screaming Beatles fans after they'd been to a Beatles concert. Edwina had taught Lisa the Liverpool accent, and it was so cool.

Helmut did a strong-man *Star Trek* act with Tak.

Miss Cappelli, Lisa, and Chook's was really clever. It was ex! An alphabet poem with something funny about every single person at camp. We're going to get a copy.

Then the Miners did a leech number with their sleeping bags pulled up to their necks. That was cool, too. They were all gourmet leeches, swaying around, talking about their best meals.

It was a great show, but most people thought the pirates were the best. Jonah's song was the hot topic.

The Convicts helped push the couches back, so we were about the last ones walking in the dark back to the dining hut for cake. From behind the blacksmith's, The Bomb stepped out in front of Jonah. We got a hell of a fright, but Jonah stood rock still.

"You're very close to the edge, boy," growled The Bomb.

Jonah was mad. His eyes blazed. "You're not a *teacher!*"

Mitch and I grabbed his arms and tried to drag him.

"You make everybody *miserable…*" Jonah flung the words at The Bomb. "*…including yourself!*"

We ran.

!!!!!

I woke in a sweat of fear. Night. More noises. A bed creaked. Dead scary. Like a horror movie. It was dark, but I could just make out Jonah, crouching motionless inside the tent flap, holding his heavy flashlight high with both hands, like he was going to whack somebody with it. He saw I was awake.

"Somebody's out there," he breathed.

I was scared by him being so scared, and the noise, the dark, and the strangeness.

"Somebody going to the toilet?"

Jonah brought his arms down a bit. "Don't think so."

I could hear the scuffling, too. We parted the flap a fraction and peered out into the night.

It was Mary taking the wombats and the wallaby for their run. We could see shapes quite clearly.

"What are you kids doing awake?" She looked at us. Well,

really, she looked at Jonah. "Come, too," she said quietly. "Quick! Grab a sweater!"

The animals were racing up the hill.

We didn't talk. We followed them through the darkness. The air was cold on my face. I wished I'd put socks on. The animals trotted ahead, dark blobs on the ground. We left the track and scrambled, cracking and crunching through the thin bush, till we came to a hollow with a dry creek bed. The little wallaby was bouncing around. Bulldozer and Thornton Primary snuffled happily.

It was like a dream: the dark shapes of the animals, the bush smell, the cold air. We sat on a fallen tree trunk and watched the animals, in silence at first. Then Mary, speaking in a low voice that was like part of the night, told us about the animals. "They find a place where there are no droppings from other wombats, and that becomes their patch, where I take them night after night. What happened in the river today, Jonah?" Mary slipped in the question quietly, as if it was simply the next thing to say.

Jonah was silent.

"You can trust me," said Mary in her slow, soothing voice, "and Mark and the wombats won't say a word."

We sat quietly for what seemed like ages. Thornton Primary, snuffling around, made a skittering run at Bulldozer, who lost his balance and toppled over. It was funny. The little wallaby jumped straight up in the air.

Softly, Jonah started to talk. "I was looking forward to canoeing. I've never been in a canoe before. Then The Bomb turned up. Everyone picked partners fast, and I was left on my own. He hates me, but Mandy, who was in charge, didn't know that."

"Sorry, Jonah," I mumbled. He went on as if he didn't hear me.

"The canoe was in the water, and The Bomb quickly got in the back seat. I had no chance. I had to get into the front. I was scared and sweating.

"It was going okay, then we played a game and Chris's hat fell into the water near us. There was a fair current…you could feel it. I reached out with my paddle for the hat, then—so fast—we shot round the bend.

"I looked behind, and The Bomb had his paddle in the air. I thought, If he bashes me there would be no proof. He would say I hit a rock. I was scared stiff. The river got faster and louder. He was paddling hard. The canoe shot along like an arrow. 'Will we get that hat, Sonny Jim?' he yelled.

"I tried to steer into the slower part of the river, but he was paddling hard against me, splashing me. Then I saw the old railway bridge up ahead.

"'There's the bridge, Sonny Jim,'" he yelled. He gave a hard paddle and spun the canoe around and we were flying backward so *fast!* And rocking! He didn't care! I thought, He's trying to get both of us drowned. I was terrified.

"The river got narrower, and the water was roaring and foaming between big rocks. The canoe half swung round, bumped and bashed about, like things were punching it from under the water. I was trying hard to stay in. 'Not scared are you, Sonny Jim?' he yelled.

"Then—smash! We hit an underwater rock. The back end of the canoe flicked up, and I was half out. I lost my paddle, and the canoe was on its side, then it was straight again…and he wasn't sitting behind me anymore."

Jonah stopped and moved a little. I was shivering, hardly breathing.

"What happened then?" said Mary carefully, quietly.

"The canoe got jammed by the pounding water between two big rocks, like the middle bar of an H. I jumped like a grasshopper onto a rock. Looking back through a gap, I could just see The Bomb's leg. I leapt from rock to rock till I could see him properly. He was being pushed by the water into a fallen tree. His head was going under, bobbing up and down. He looked like he was nodding...unconscious.

"I didn't know what to do. I wedged a stick between the rocks, underneath his head, so his head stopped nodding. It was tipped back, as if he was gazing at the sky. Except his eyes were closed. But he hadn't gone blue or anything.

"He was so heavy. And the current was strong. I couldn't move him.

"On the side of the river there was a track and an old truck, with fishing gear. The keys were under the dash. I got a rope around him, started up the truck, and dragged him out.

"He was coming and going. I thought he'd had the gong. His eyes would be back in his head, then he'd look like he was asleep. Then I turned, and he was watching me."

Jonah stopped again. He shifted on the log and tried to clear his throat, as if the words were stuck in it. We sat in fragile silence.

"Jonah, my dear," said Mary, "if you don't talk about a problem, it grows. Keep talking. It will help."

Jonah took a deep breath. "I left him there...crossed the bridge and walked back to camp. I thought...If he lives, he lives, if he dies he dies...Some things have to die, you know," he said in a matter-of-fact voice.

"I had a dog," he said as if the story went on. "She was a kelpie, black with little tan spots over her eyes. When we were leaving the farm I gave her to another farmer, but he had to keep her on the chain because she kept running back. She wouldn't stay, so the farmer said he didn't want her. She wouldn't come to anyone but me.

"The last weekend before we left our farm, I got a lift and took her right out of the valley, a long way away. I took off her collar and let her go beside the road. I was sure somebody would pick her up and keep her, she was so beautiful, so smart. She was too smart. She found her way home before we left for the city."

Jonah's voice went funny. "She was my best friend. We had to shoot her." With a little sob he ducked his head, twisted off the log, and stumbled into the bush.

The animals stopped, alert at the sudden movement.

"Poor, poor soul," sighed Mary.

I felt so heavy and sad for him. "Will I go and find him, Mary?"

"No, just wait," she said.

A while later, sure enough, we heard snapping sticks, and the dark shape of Jonah came out of the bush. He blew his nose on his sleeve. "Don't tell anybody."

"You're holding a lot of secrets, aren't you, Jonah?" said Mary quietly.

Jonah nodded.

In the first soft light of morning, we walked back to camp.

36 ALL BAD THINGS COME TO AN END

"Hey, guys! Hey, *guys! HEY, GUYS!*" Azza pounded up the hill.

"Are we in trouble?" goes Wormz.

"HEY, GUYS! You won't *believe* it! *THE BOMB'S GONE!*"

What happened last night? Or was it morning? I saw one of my shoes by the tent flap, then Jonah's story rushed into my head.

It was true. Mr. Brian "The Bomb" Cromwell was gone. The little hut was empty. The car with the scratch gone.

There was a strange feeling about the place. Something mysterious had happened.

The lovely Miss Cappelli was snappy. She was on the phone to school, telling them about the peculiar situation. I wonder if she told them about Jonah's song. Naomi said it was the Convicts who caused it. But the strangeness didn't last for long.

"The Bomb has gone!" said Nicko. "Get real!" He ripped off Jonah's hat and threw it high in the air.

"Whaleman," grinned Mitch, "this is the first day of the rest of your life!"

37 RE-ENTRY

We packed up, shoving all our stuff and everybody else's, wet, dry, clean, and dirty, into our bags. Chook held up various disgusting wet objects from a pile of lost property a meter high. Lisa and Edwina swapped addresses. We took last photos.

"On behalf of grade 5/6, I'd like to thank you, Mary, for showing us how the pioneers lived and how you help animals get back to the wild again, and Helmut for helping us with the activities, and Edwina for the fantastic food. We had a really great time," said Faith Williamson.

"Three cheers for Gumbinya!" yelled Lisa.

"Hip, hip, HOORAY!!!!!!!

"Hip, hip, HOOORAAAAAAAY!!!!!

"Hip, hip, HOOOOORAAAAAAAAAAAAAAAAAAAAAAY!!!!!!"

Mary gave a big smile. "One thing I know I'm going to miss is this hat!" And she whipped Jonah's hat off his head and tried it on. Then she pulled a face, as if to say, it doesn't suit me. As she put it back on his head, she gave him a quick little hug and whispered something. Not that anybody else would notice. But for Jonah and me it had meaning.

！！！！！

Nicko saved us good seats at the back of the bus.

"I just want to have fish and chips and watch TV," said Wormz, flopping down in his seat.

Mitch was last on. He tossed a plastic bag of wet clothes at Jonah. "You left them in the showers."

"Thanks," said Jonah.

"That's okay," said Mitch. "You just have to be eternally grateful."

Waving good-bye and looking back from the bus, I saw Mary standing alone. I mean, Helmut and Edwina were there, but she seemed to be by herself. I thought about her life. Everybody came to Mary, and then they left. The animals went back to the bush, the kids went home, Helmut and Edwina would go back to their countries. Did Mary get lonely? Did she have someone to hang on to? I suppose she had Mintie and Little Petal. Well, Little Petal would be a good friend, but I wouldn't bank on Mintie.

I tried to imagine Mary in a house in the city. No way!

I thought of her in the early morning, taking the wombats home to the creek bed. I looked at Jonah, and I suddenly felt sure Jonah would go back to the bush, too. In a way, by her quiet questions, Mary was easing Jonah back to his place, just like the wombats. I don't think Jonah would have told his story to anybody else. And even after all The Bomb did to him, I never, never, never saw him cry before.

Most people float around, stay awhile here, stay awhile there. Does it matter if you don't have a place? What's my place? I thought.

Sitting on the bus, I felt fragile, like an eggshell with no egg inside it. I was keeping the biggest secret I'd ever kept.

Did The Bomb really try to kill Jonah?

Watching the trees and the fences and the posts and the road, my eyes were looking at them, but my mind wasn't. Sitting next to Jonah. He didn't say a thing. Just stared out of the window, too.

It was hard knowing something that everybody else didn't

know. Especially when they were all talking about it, and guessing, and their guesses were wrong.

There was so much I wondered about. I remembered Mary asking him, "You're holding a lot of secrets, aren't you?" and Jonah nodding. The story of his dog made me cry whenever I thought of it. So I had to be careful not to think of it. If ever I'm an actor in the movies and I have to cry, it will be easy. I'll just think of Jonah and his dog.

What other secrets did Jonah have locked inside him?

"Can you really drive a car?" I asked.

Jonah nodded. "And tractor, and truck." He told me about their farm. Their house was a long way from the road where he had to catch the school bus, so his dad fixed up an old VW. He welded some metal to the pedals to make them longer, so Jonah's feet could reach them, and he extended the gear lever. Jonah drove himself to the road every morning and home every night.

The bus was pretty quiet. Nobody was singing. They were staring out the window. Thinking. Dreaming. Wondering. Asleep. Hard to believe it was only five days since camp began. Rocking smoothly along in the warm bus, with the steady drone of the engine. Looking at the rows and rows of pine trees through the window. So tired.

I woke up with Rebecca yelling, "Hey, that's the street where my auntie lives!"

We were not far from school, back to shops and houses, streets, trash cans, traffic lights, cars, supermarkets, families...

We were home again.

I was so tired.

38 AFTER THE HOLIDAYS

The holidays began straight after camp.

We never saw The Bomb again. We heard he was working in a hardware shop in Bendigo. We heard he was in Kings Cross in Sydney, working in one of those Adults Only shops. We heard he got a job on a boat going to Singapore. Someone said they saw him at Camberwell Trash and Treasure Market.

He didn't even go back to school to collect his stuff, not that he had much anyway. And our projects on the planets, that he'd had for over six weeks, were given back without him even looking at them.

When it was officially announced at assembly that Mr. Cromwell had left the staff, Mitch yelled out *"Hallelujah!"* and it spread, until for a crazy minute all the kids were yelling *"HALLELUJAH!!!!!!"*

And Adrian got a new teacher—Mrs. Beagley. We were worried at first, because she said things like, "I'm mean, and I'm nasty, and I've told you ninety-seven times," but she turned out funny. Nearly as good as Miss Cappelli.

At the end of the holidays, I rummaged for my Mambo pencil case in the junk from camp that I'd dumped in the corner of my room. There was something wrapped around the pencil case—a friendship band made out of Mintie's wool. Jonah had finished it off with a neat sliding knot and put it there for me.

I wasn't surprised to hear that Jonah had gone, too. He left our school as suddenly as he arrived. We heard that his family went back to work on his uncle's farm. I hope so. The name Tubbut meant Jonah for me. It sounded like a hard stubborn nut. Well, he was a Coconut for a while.

"It's a funny thing," said Nicko. "You wouldn't think you'd miss anybody who didn't say much or do anything, would you?"

"What was the last thing Jonah said to us?" goes Wormz.

"'Thanks,'" said Mitch.

"Could have been more interesting than that, don't you reckon?" said Azza.

"Like what?"

"Something more important...like..."

"Like?"

"I dunno."

!!!!!

But that wasn't quite the end.

The first morning back at school, I had to take the lunch orders down. Heather in the office was pounding away at the computer. She glanced up, over her glasses.

"Ah, Mark, just the one I want to see," she said, still pounding away. "What's Jonah's new address?"

"Don't know. Sorry."

"No matter. I thought he might have told you. We'll send it to his old address, and they'll forward it on."

Then I noticed a long brown packet lying on her desk, addressed to Jonah. I picked it up. It had DO NOT BEND written on it.

I looked closer. It was The Bomb's writing, I'm sure. I could feel a long piece of cardboard, and on top of it I could feel something else.

I swear it was a feather.

142

Also available from Yearling Books

Everybody knows Crash Coogan, seventh-grade football sensation. He's been mowing down everything in his path since the time he could walk—and Penn Webb, his dweeby, vegetable-eating neighbor, is his favorite target. After all, Webb's not just a nerd, he's a cheerleader, too.

Crash and his best buddy, Mike, can't think of anything more hilarious than making Webb's life miserable. But Crash starts to realize that Webb has something he may never gain, no matter how many touchdowns he scores. And when Mike takes a prank too far, maybe even for Crash, the football star has to choose which side he's really on.

"Spinelli packs a powerful moral wallop, leaving it to the pitch-perfect narration to drive home his point." —*Publishers Weekly*

★"Readers will devour this humorous glimpse of what jocks are made of."   —*School Library Journal*, Starred

Winner of ten state Children's Choice awards
An ALA Best Book for Young Adults
A *School Library Journal* Best Book of the Year